Reunions Can Be Murder

D1523046

By Tammy Wunsch

Dedications and Thanks

Thank you to all the people who helped me edit this book – Elizabeth Upp and Susan Herrick for your invaluable editing skills and to Gwen Sanchirico for her final proofread.

Thank you also to Margaret Schramke for the cover design and to Kate Duffy for the Kat Snow logo.

Continued appreciation to my friends who helped me choose a title for the book through my Google Poll on Facebook.

Finally, a HUGE thank-you to all my readers, friends, and family for all your encouragement. Without your support, these would just be words on a paper.

I hope you enjoy this new series. Any resemblance to persons or places – either living or dead – is purely coincidental. This is a work of fiction and is not based on any actual events.

So, grab a glass of wine and happy reading!

P.S., Don't forget the two bonuses in the back of the book!

Suggested wines (which will be tasted by the characters):
- *Rias Baixas Albariño*
- Dakota Sky Vineyard Cabernet Sauvignon
- Mumm, DVX Reserves
- Beringer Chardonnay Napa Valley Reserve
- Domaine Chandon Brut Napa County Cuvée 494 Reserve
- Cornerstone Corallina Rosé Stepping Stone Napa Valley
- Chateau Montelena Estate Cabernet Sauvignon Napa Valley
- Paul Hobbs Chardonnay

Table of Contents

Chapter One

"We are SO going to that reunion!" Syd wasn't usually so forceful but her tone of voice made Ricky and me look at each other and burst into laughter.

"As if," Ricky snorted, trying to regain his breath.

Sydney looked peeved, then got a mischievous glint in her eyes and pretended to pout. "Please? I really, really, really want to go," she whined.

I looked at her again and wondered, what is she planning?

Sydney "Syd" Randall, née Miller, was not usually manipulative. Long, wavy black hair, green eyes, coffee-colored skin, and a figure that most women would kill for, she was also the nicest, sweetest, and most loyal best friend anyone could ask for. We had been next-door neighbors and best friends our whole lives. We made tree forts together, cut each other's hair (to our parents' chagrin), drank our first beer together (and later threw up together), and double-dated for prom. She married Ty Randall – the high school quarterback – right after graduation and moved to Rhode Island. Away from me. Okay, she had a full scholarship to the Rhode Island School of Design and Ty went to URI on a football scholarship, and, it was only one and a half-hours away – but that felt like a million miles after she had lived next-door to me since birth.

They eventually moved back to Harmony – that's where we grew up – about an hour north of Boston, not too far from Plum Island. They moved back about five years ago when Ty took over the job of Chief of Police of Harmony. He had risen in the ranks in Providence and it was a great move for the family. Syd opened an art gallery that did a great business in the summer with all the tourists in the harbor area and she was able to focus on her own art in the off season. She also worked as a graphic designer to fund her passions and had made quite a name for herself. I think every shop in Harmony had hired her to update their logos and marketing materials.

They have three kids though they're practically adults now. The twins, Tayler and Ty Jr. are 20 and away at different colleges in Boston. Sarah is 18 and a pianist prodigy. She will graduate from a special music school on Plum Island this year and I don't think she's decided what to do next, though she's been approached by the Royal Academy of Music in London and the Juilliard School of Performing Arts in New York.

I glanced at Ricky quickly to make sure he was still breathing and saw he had settled into a comfortable chuckle.

Riku "Ricky" Tanaka became my second best friend in seventh grade when he told Amelia Smythe-Jones (Smythe is pronounced with a long "I" and she was as pretentious as her name) to shut her narcissistic, artificial nose and her counterfeit Gucci bag and go back to the hole she climbed out of. Amelia was in the middle of ridiculing me and calling me "white trash" because my mother owned the local dive bar, The Harbor Bar. He earned my eternal gratitude and unending friendship that day as Amelia slunk back to her lunch table with mean boys and girls. Ricky was every Asian stereotype you could fit into one person. He was brilliant at math and computers, obsessed with animé and could barely drive two blocks without knocking over a trash can or hitting a curb. He was also the most stunningly beautiful drag queen I had ever seen. Not that he walked around dressed in drag. Not every day. Most of the time, he was just a nerd who designed MMORPG (Massive Multiplayer Online Role-Playing Games, for the uninformed) and made a boatload of money. After high school, though, he deserted me, too. He also got a full scholarship, but to MIT. He was then recruited by some video game company in his junior year after developing some new way of making virtual reality more real.

2

He's still single, too, so it's nice to have someone to pal around with on Saturday nights – when he's not in drag. I just hate it when he's prettier than me.

Ricky had bought out a small video game company in Cold Harbor, two towns away. He already doubled the business and published an amazing MMRPG, *Call of the Wild*, which has to do with rescuing animals in hazardous situations. I've only made it to level three but Syd's son Ty Jr. has already made it to level 20 and he told me it just gets better and better. Kids are definitely more skilled at these games than adults. Ricky lives in one of the cute condos in the newly–gentrified area of the marina with three bedrooms, an open-concept living space, and a water view from the large balcony. I guess you know where we hang out when we just want to drink wine and feel the ocean breeze on our faces. Ricky's parents want him to move back to Japan with the rest of the family, but he seems very content here in Harmony.

As I mentioned, we all live in Harmony again, our quaint little hometown near the New Hampshire border. My friends left for an education and ambitious goals. I left to escape my life and the grim future I saw for myself in this town, hoping for something at least a little better. I had dreams of a nicer life – for a while, at least.

Until last year happened. A dark year. An unhappy year filled with pain and misery and the shattering of dreams.

At least I still have my friends.

Chapter Two

Hi! I'm Kat Snow and I'm, well, I don't really know what I am anymore. Growing up, everyone called me Kat and I thought that was fine. After I graduated high school, I reinvented myself as Katrina. This worked out well for me until Hurricane Katrina decimated New Orleans and much of Louisiana and Florida in 2005. I got tired of the jokes and comments so transformed myself back to Kat.

I'm just an average gal. In the right light, past boyfriends have said I look a little bit like a young Sharon Stone. I have the blonde hair and blue eyes, but I'm certainly not movie star glamorous. I'll leave that to Syd and Ricky, especially when he's in drag. I used to be athletic, until last year, that is…

As I mentioned earlier, I escaped Harmony after my two best friends left me for their bright futures. I wasn't academically brilliant or artistically gifted so there were no scholarships for me. I was just your average, small-town girl who needed to get away from her alcoholic mother who drank as much as she sold at the dive bar she owned. I decided, in a moment of desperation, to join the army. The first year was tough, as my rebellious nature bucked at the forced structure, discipline, and will of the institution. Then, one day, I got it. It made sense. The army was now my family. I threw myself whole-heartedly into my career. I became a military police officer and re-upped when my first tour was over.

I retired from the army after eight years – tired of the sun and fun of the desert – and moved to Boston. I loved law enforcement so I joined the BPD, more commonly known as the Boston Police Department. I did well and earned outstanding reviews and multiple commendations. Two years ago, I made detective and was assigned to Homicide. My partner and I got along great and we made some high-profile busts. I felt satisfied about myself and the job I was doing. Then, a year ago, a meth addict in Roxbury jumped out from a darkened doorway and stabbed me ten times before my partner pulled him off of me. I nearly died and part of one lung had to be removed. It has been a long, painful recovery and the doctors determined that I would never recover enough to rejoin the BPD, so I was discharged on disability. I had been dedicated to physical therapy, but some hurdles are insurmountable.

In the middle of trying to decide what to do with the rest of my life, my mother succumbed to her various illnesses – alcoholism, emphysema, you name it – and left me the bar. The last thing I wanted to do was to be the owner of The Harbor Bar in Harmony. That place nearly sucked the life out of me as a kid. I didn't want it to happen again as an adult. I put the bar up for sale and surprisingly had an offer within a week. I hear the new owners have cleaned it up nicely. Apparently, they turned it into a combination wine bar, coffee shop, and lounge and the grand opening was coming up in a few weeks.

I also inherited my mother's house – the house I grew up in. When I first walked in, after gagging on the smoke-permeated air, I saw the nice things about the house I had never noticed as a kid. It was in a desirable neighborhood on a hillside, with a fantastic view of Harmony's harbor from the backyard. I was determined to leave Harmony and knew it wouldn't sell "as-is," so I recruited my two besties and we renovated the house. The physical exertion helped my recovery by keeping me active and engaged.

Ricky invited me to stay with him while we renovated the house, which seemed like a good decision. First, we removed the wallpaper saturated by my mother's forty-year, three-pack-a-day habit. Next, we pulled up the bits of cheap, chipped linoleum that had somehow survived all these years and marveled at the beautiful hardwood we found underneath. I sprayed some chemicals on the walls and floors that the hardware store guy recommended to remove the smoke stench. We kept the windows open for a week and now you can't smell even a hint of smoke. With the odor gone, we put up some beadboard and painted the house in cheery, beachy colors. I converted the third bedroom into a walk-in closet and master bath with a shower big enough for six people (not that I'd ever want to test that out). We updated the appliances and installed French doors going out to the stone patio – did I mention that Ricky also is a master mason? – with a huge Jacuzzi, massive gas grill, cozy sitting area with a chiminea, and a comfortable dining area.

I had planned to sell, but once we were done, it looked so nice and my two best friends lived within a mile of the house – my house, I now call it – so I decided to stay for a while.

I still didn't know what my next career move would be but I thought I could figure that out in Harmony as easily as anywhere else. I was getting by on disability but I really thought I would go crazy if I didn't find a job to keep my mind occupied – video games were not going to be enough for me. I was pretty sure my two best friends could help me figure out my life, like they helped me renovate my house, and then maybe I could find my dream job, now that law enforcement was off the table. Stupid meth addicts!

Little did I know that circumstances and coincidences, not my best friends – would decide my fate – and it all had to do with Syd wanting to go to that damn high school reunion.

Chapter Three

Syd got her way, just like she always does. The whining and sulking were just too much for Ricky and me. She also confessed that she wanted to rub Amelia's (fake) nose in the fact that she was a working artist and gallery owner, not to mention a highly successful graphic artist. More on Amelia later but suffice to say, she was one of our high school nemeses. Amelia had once called Syd a no-talent hack in art class and her vicious friends had all laughed at her. They say revenge is a dish best served cold – in this case, 20 years cold!

The reunion was being held at the Harmony Resort. The Reunion Committee had blocked off a rooms for classmates for the gathering. Even though we lived locally, the three of us pitched in for a room. We figured it would be nice to meet up with people and bounce around from room to room at before- and after–parties. Ty wanted none of the excess social frivolity and opted out of our shared hotel room. He was a year ahead of us in school, so he wasn't part of our class. The weekend was booked solid with activities and get-togethers and we planned to use our weekend to indulge in some of the spa packages for guests.

I checked in on Friday afternoon. Syd and Ricky were coming after they finished work for the day but I wanted to beat the rush. As I walked through the door of the resort, I spied a table with a banner that read "Welcome Harmony High School Class of 2000!" I headed over and picked up the weekend's agenda when I heard a shrill voice exclaim, "Kat! Look what you dragged in," as if I had never heard that particular joke before.

My back stiffened and I slowly turned around, agenda in hand. I unclenched my teeth into a semblance of a smile. "Amelia Smythe-Jones, you're here," was literally the only not negative thing I could think of to say.

"It's Amelia Smythe-Jones-Beauregard now, dear. I married Robert Beauregard. You remember? His family owned this resort?"

Why was she saying everything to me in the form of a question? Was I on Jeopardy? Oh hell, now I'm doing it! I shook my head and thought, leave it to Amelia Smythe-Jones to marry Bo Beauregard and just extend her hyphenated name. Like Smythe-Jones wasn't long enough? Oh crap, I'm still doing it!

Thinking of Bo made me smile. He was one of the few people in this town who never looked down at me for being the local barkeep's daughter. He even took me to junior prom. "How is Bo? Is he managing the resort now?" I looked around as if I might see him in the lobby.

Amelia cleared her throat. "It's Robert now. He outgrew his silly nickname when we graduated high school, unlike other people." She gave me a pointed look. I was about to launch into the whole Katrina saga but she continued her speech, "The Harmony Resort is now part of Consolidated Resorts International. When we decided to sell the property, they offered Robert a position as Director of Domestic Operations. He has now moved up to Vice President of Operations and we're very happy. We live in Upper Harmony now?" She ended her speech, again with a non-question question, and gave me a self-satisfied smile as if his achievements were only accomplished because of her. Upper Harmony was, as its name suggested, located above the town of Harmony – both in attitude and latitude – although, funnily enough, just one street away from my house.

I swallowed my negativity and managed to croak out, "How very nice for you?" I managed to pose it in the form of a question. Two can play this Jeopardy game, so there.

She was still smiling like the Cheshire cat and leaned in to pat my arm. "As you probably know, I'm the top real estate broker in Harmony and Upper Harmony? I *only* deal in exclusive properties."

I hardly had reason to know anything about anyone in this town or to consider the buying or selling of an "exclusive property," but I had seen her face on bus stops so I knew what she did for a living. I managed a nod and tried to move around her to check in.

Amelia side-stepped in front of me and stage-whispered, "How are you, Kat? I hear that you were in the army?" She looked me up and down as if I had ventured into the resort in my dirty cammies.

I had had enough of her condescension. "Yes, I was part of the military police helping to maintain order for our troops. Then I moved to Boston and was a detective in the homicide division."

She nodded sympathetically. "Yes, I heard you got into a tussle with the criminal element and were forced out of the department?"

Damn that questioning tone. I threw back my shoulders and took a step toward Amelia Smythe-Jones-Beauregard. "I retired on disability after a drug dealer and addict stabbed me ten times, destroyed one of my lungs, and served no time in prison, even though I nearly died."

Amelia took a step back and her hand fluttered up to her mouth. "Well, I, er, am happy you recovered enough to attend our reunion?" She noticed the agenda in my hand. "Make sure you sign up for 'Wine Tasting' at 3:00 tomorrow. You surely remember that Marco Milano's family owns the Milano Vineyard so he has such in-depth wine knowledge. He runs the family vineyard and he launched Milano Fine Wines to import quality wines from around the world. His office and warehouse are at the family vineyard so he can help out when they need him. We will be featuring wines that Marco has recommended this weekend at the resort and Marco is going to have a tasting of some wines he hand-picked personally. It

9

should be a lot of fun?" She nodded enthusiastically, warming to her topic, "You remember Marco? He was on the football team and he and I used to date in high school?"

I frowned. Marco had been Amelia's boyfriend freshman year of high school and had dated a lot of girls, though he never seemed to notice me or Syd. "I'm not getting a clear picture of him?" Two could play this game and I was a master. "Excuse me while I check in and sign up for some of the events." I turned my back on her and felt her hesitate behind me. She finally turned around and walked toward the front desk, calling out enthusiastically to some other poor soul.

The agenda for the Harmony High Class of 2000 Reunion certainly was packed full of events and opportunities for meeting, greeting, and drinking. The agenda was in a glossy brochure (that Syd had designed) and was loaded with coupons and advertisements for local businesses – Smythe-Jones-Beauregard Realtors featured prominently. Regardless of my reluctance to attend the reunion, it could be a fun weekend, despite Amelia and all her non-questions.

Harmony High School Y2K Reunion
Weekend Agenda

Friday:	Time & Location
Welcome Reception	6:30-7:00 p.m.
Wine provided by Milano Importers	Green Room
Welcome Dinner	7:00-9:00 p.m.
*Welcome Remarks, Cal Mercury, Jr.	Harbor View Restaurant
*Itinerary Review, Amelia S-J-B	
*Musical Performance, Alumni Band	
Drinks and Dancing	9:00-11:00 p.m.
	Harbor View Lounge
After-Hours Parties	11:00-?
Locations posted on Facebook invite	

Saturday:

Reunion Wake-Up Breakfast	8:00-9:00 a.m.
	Breakfast Nook
Seaside Yoga	9:00-9:30 a.m.
*Sponsored by Harbor Resort	Yoga Platform/Pool
Y2K-Themed Obstacle Course	10:00-11:30 a.m.
*Sponsored by Robert & Amelia	Tennis Courts
*Spectacular prizes!	
Classmates Memorial	11:30-12:00 p.m.
	Green Room
Recognition Luncheon	1:00-2:30 p.m.
*Sponsored by Alumni Association	Harbor Restaurant Patio

Harmony High School
Y2K Reunion Weekend

YOUR CHOICE – Pick 1 OF 4

1. Iron Man Fitness Class with Cal Mercury, Jr.	3:00-4:00 p.m.
*Sponsored by The Mercury	Great Lawn
2. Author Talk and Book Signing	3:00-4:00 p.m.
*Presented by MJ Cromwell	Green Room
3. Advertising with Advanced Games	3:00–4:00 p.m.
*Presented by Riku Tanaka	Sunset Room
4. Wine Talk and Tasting	3:00–4:00 p.m.
*Presented by Milano Wine Importers	Blue Room

High Tea by Harmony Resort	4:30-5:30 p.m.
*Pastries by Sunny Side Up Bakery	Lounge Patio

Happy Hour	6:00-7:00 p.m.
*Reunion Photos	Harmony Resort Lounge

Dinner, Drinks, & Dancing	7:30-11:00 p.m.
Festivities include:	Harmony Resort Ballroom
*Reunion Photos (cont'd)	
*Yearbook review	

After-Hours Parties	11:00-?
Locations posted on Facebook invite	

Sunday:

Reunion Wake-Up Breakfast	8:00-9:00 a.m.
	Breakfast Nook

School Club Reunions	9:30-10:30 a.m.
	Blue Room

Ice Cream Social	10:30-11:30 a.m.
*Presented by Harmony Dairy	Lounge Patio
*Signing of Reunion Memory Books	

End of Reunion Luncheon	12:00-1:00 p.m.
*Resort Check Out	Harbor View Restaurant

Chapter Four

I was sitting in our hotel room with a nice glass of merlot when Syd and Ricky joined me at 6:00 p.m. They were delighted to see the two-bedroom suite in which I was currently silently fuming. Syd took one look at my rigid face and sighed. "What's the matter?"

I sat up and glared around the spacious suite, extending my arms outward. "This! I booked a double room at the resort. After 'catching up' – " I used air quotes, which I generally hate, with Amelia Smythe-Jones-Beauregard at the check-in table, she went to the front desk and had them upgrade us to a suite."

"How do you know it was her?" asked Ricky who was peering into the extra-large guest bathroom. "Wait, what? Amelia Smythe-Jones-Beauregard? Can she hyphenate a few more names onto her name?"

I welcomed Ricky's solidarity. "Right?" Then, I sputtered, "How do I know? How do I know?" Damn, I was still doing it. "She told them to let me know that we were upgraded courtesy of the Beaureagards, and that the entire weekend would be comped." I shook my head and looked around the elegant suite, muttering, "Like we can't pay for our own suite."

Syd laughed and I glared at her.

"You're an idiot," she shook her finger at me.

"What? Why?"

"If Amelia wants to make herself feel by paying for our weekend, I say let her feel superior. We get to spread out and really pamper ourselves—for free!"

As I opened my mouth to protest, Syd cocked her eye at a menu of services, "Will you be having one massage or two this weekend, Ms. Snow?" She then picked up a room service menu and turned to Ricky.

"Mr. Tanaka, I see they have that expensive caviar you love and usually only get on super-special occasions. One jar or two?"

I paused for a second and reset my mind-frame when I understood her devious plan. Then, I leaned across the back of the couch and picked up the phone and asked for room service.

"Please send up a bottle – no make it two – of Dom Perignon, please. Chilled. With three glasses. And two jars of caviar as well. Thank you."

Syd and Ricky threw themselves on the couch next to me and we convulsed with laughter as we waited for our Dom and perused the weekend's agenda.

Having missed the Welcome Reception due to our own bubbly-filled reception in our room—no, suite—we stumbled a little on our way down to dinner, giggling like schoolgirls. As we stepped off the elevator, we walked right into Marla Jean Cromwell. At least, that's what her name tag said, although she didn't look anything like the Marla Jean Cromwell we knew in high school.

Marla Jean had been a very shy classmate. Her parents ran a dairy outside of town and Marla Jean and her brothers and sisters – there were five or six of them, I can never remember them all – helped them out before and after school. She couldn't participate much in school activities but she had always been nice to me. We were in a few classes together and I always made sure to sit near her, two outcasts in a storm. To say Marla Jean had changed was an understatement. In high school, she was thin as a rail with mousy brown hair and slightly buck teeth. She always wore threadbare hand-me-downs from her older sisters. She wasn't ugly, but she wasn't pretty, either.

The woman I saw today looked nothing like the teenage Marla Jean I remembered from high school. She was still slim, but she was at least a D cup, if not a DD or larger. I wasn't even sure how she could stand upright. Her hair was dyed platinum blonde and fell in soft waves to her shoulders. The dress she had on was definitely from a designer I had never heard of and fit her new curves like a glove. Her make-up looked professionally applied and when she smiled, her teeth were now perfectly sized and as white as I had ever seen on anyone. "Marla Jean?" I inquired, unsure if it was really her and not some distant relative.

Her smile was a little disdainful. "It's MJ now, Kat."

Suddenly, everything fell into place like a giant puzzle. MJ Cromwell was the name of an author of a risqué series of books having to do with love, bondage, and subservience. I don't know why I had never put it together before that MJ Cromwell was actually *Marla Jean* Cromwell from Harmony. Her books had sold millions of copies all around the world and had been made into successful movies with famous actors. I had even bought the first book and blushed my way through reading it alone during my recovery. I think my mouth hung open from the shock.

She finally grinned. "Stop, Kat. It's still me. It's just that now, I'm a best-selling author."

I gulped. "Uhm, well, I sat next to you in English class and I don't remember you enjoying writing all that much." Actually, I didn't think I had ever seen her open a book and had never been sure if she could even read.

She leaned in and purred in my ear, "It depends on the subject matter." She then giggled and gave a little wave as she strutted off in four-inch stilettos toward the dining room.

15

Syd and I followed slowly, feeling very under-dressed in our black skirts, twin sets, and sensible heels. Even Ricky looked plain and boring, not elegant, in his monochromatic black slacks, shirt, and jacket with a custom-made tie from Japan. He stood there agape for a moment watching her walk away, then rushed to catch up with us.

"Girls, we need to step up our game." He stood in front of us with his hands on his hips. "It is time for some designer duds and classy accessories."

I thought about my quickly dwindling bank account. "I'll be fine with what I brought."

Ricky grinned maliciously. "Have you forgotten? This weekend is entirely on the Beauregards." He pointed to the lobby which housed some exclusive boutiques. "I see our new outfits right in that boutique and I'm sure Amelia and Bo would want us to feel and look fabulous, relaxed, and completely satisfied with our experience!"

Syd and I burst out laughing, our spirits rejuvenated. We each took one of Ricky's arms and marched triumphantly into the dining room, whispering "Tomorrow, we shop!"

Chapter Five

Syd, Ricky, and I entered the dining room and started searching for seats. Unfortunately, because we were so late, most of the tables had already filled up. Ty waved to us from a table by the bar. The three of us made our way over but there was only one seat remaining. Syd stamped her foot.

"Ty, you were supposed to save us seats," she said crossly.

He shrugged. "And you were supposed to be here thirty minutes ago. I just got here myself and you're lucky I was able to save *you* a seat." He shrugged apologetically at me and Ricky.

Ricky fist-bumped Ty. "No problem, dude. We were catching up and making plans for the weekend. Syd will fill you in on our good fortune." He hooked his arm through mine and said in a sing-song tone, "We'll let the lovebirds sit together." Syd punched him gently on the arm and he smirked at her as he pulled me along. "Let's go find a seat."

Syd slipped into the available seat and called out to our departing backs, "Meet you after dessert!"

As soon as we took a few steps, I heard people shouting out Ricky's name. We turned toward a table at the rear of the restaurant and Ricky started grinning from ear to ear. He smiled at me. "It's my friends from the Robotics Club." The table of men was beckoning Ricky over. Ricky shrugged apologetically. "I could try to find you a seat at the table but you would probably be bored. Most of those guys are programmers and they are ALL serious gamers. They will probably grill me about *Call of the Wild*."

I rolled my eyes and disengaged my arm from Ricky's. "I suppose I can manage one dinner on my own."

Ricky kissed me on the cheek and nearly skipped over to his other friends. I quickly scanned the room and spied an open seat two tables away. As I got closer to the table, my heart sank. Sitting at the table were Amelia Smythe-Jones-Beauregard and her husband Bo – make that Robert – Beauregard. Amelia rested her hand possessively on Bo's – damn! Why couldn't I think of him as Robert? – bicep.

As miserable as Amelia made my life in high school, next to her was the arch-nemesis of every unpopular kid in high school, Mindy Sherwood. I couldn't even say her name without my face puckering up. She had grown up across the street from me and had always been a spoiled, rotten, mean-spirited little witch – can you tell I didn't like her? She would sneakily trip me during gym class and tried to spread rumors about me more than once. She even tried to get me expelled by claiming that she saw me cheat on the SATs. I scored so horribly they decided even if I had cheated – which I didn't – my score was punishment enough. I could never figure out why Mindy hated me so much. I guess some people are just born mean. Frankly, after high school, I had never even given a fleeting thought to Mindy Sherwood.

Next to Mindy sat a man I thought must be her husband. He was hunched over his mobile phone and busily typing away. His hair, or what was left of it, was light brown. He was wearing a wrinkled brown suit with a tan tie while Mindy was sporting a silver lamé cocktail dress, if you can believe it, and had her hair swept up into one of those hairdos that are supposed to look effortless but actually took an hour and a whole can of hairspray. She was wearing thick makeup and must have been wearing more than twenty-thousand dollars' worth of jewelry in diamond rings, bracelets, a necklace and – holy shit – she was actually wearing a tiara. She looked up and sneered, "Kat," dripping with disgust. I rubbed my sweating palms on my plain skirt and tried to hide my unadorned and

18

calloused hands. "Mindy," I replied, with as much dignity as I could muster, trying desperately not to pucker up.

Amelia clapped her hands together and exclaimed gleefully, "Oh, that's right. You two were neighbors in Upper Harmony."

Mindy cleared her throat and declared, "Kat did not live in Upper Harmony."

That's right, I lived two houses away from Upper Harmony, on the wrong side of the street. Cue my inner eye roll. Really? Shouldn't this mean girl behavior have ended after high school? Why am I still asking questions?

Amelia pretended she hadn't heard Mindy. "Kat, do you know everyone?" She looked around the table and named the other three table occupants anyway without giving me a chance to reply. "You remember Marla Jean Cromwell? She's written a few books, which were popular with a certain element." Her face scrunched up in disapproval.

MJ gritted her teeth and muttered, "It's MJ." She then turned and gave me a friendly little wave and a wink.

Amelia continued, "Next to Marl – MJ – is Sunny Mason. She owns Sunny Side Up, a bakery and tearoom on Market Street." I hadn't actually been friends with Sunny in high school, but I knew who she was. Sunny had been a cheerleader and sometimes hung out with Amelia and Mindy. She had never participated in the 'torture Kat club' and was my lab partner one year in chemistry, so I was okay with her.

Amelia had continued speaking while Sunny and I had each given the "what's up?" universal head bob. "And everyone remembers Chance Wolf. He's a lawyer in Boston now."

I felt time stand still as I turned slowly toward Chance. I felt the heat rising in my cheeks. Of course, I remembered Chance Wolf. He was every girl's – and some boys' – secret crush. Kind of a loner, he played

19

football, was captain of the swim team, and used to drive an Aston-Martin, just like James Bond. I could totally picture him in a tuxedo playing baccarat. We had been in a few classes together and once he found a note I had written to Syd signed Mrs. Kat Wolf, surrounded by hearts and about a million X's and O's. He had just grinned self-consciously and handed the note to Syd, but I had been so mortified that I avoided him for the rest of the school year.

Chance slowly rose to his feet, stepped over to me, and extended his hand. I felt mesmerized by his stunningly green eyes and shook his hand slowly. As soon as we touched, however, he bent over and kissed the top of my hand. (See, very James Bond.) With a twinkle in his eye, he turned to Amelia and said, "Kat and I know each other quite well," as he released my hand. He pulled out the empty chair next to his and I realized that I had been holding my breath. I slowly exhaled as I sat in the proffered chair. As Chance returned to his seat, I felt all eyes on me, even Mindy's phone-obsessed husband. Mindy's mouth was hanging open in a perfect "O" as she gaped at me. As I sat, I managed a weak smile and reached for my water glass. Suddenly, the room felt very warm.

Even though I was separated from my friends, I enjoyed myself quite a bit during dinner. I enjoyed Robert's – I was getting better at that – stories of guest hijinks and how people tried to scam hotels. I discovered that Mindy ran a company called Vanderbilt Culinary Catering and Events. The guy in the rumpled brown suit was indeed Mindy's husband and I heard him say that his name is Julian Vanderbilt. Mindy told Sunny she met Julian while she was at Wellesley University and he was at Harvard. I learned that he owned a finance company with a seat on the Boston Stock Exchange. While Mindy's stories about her clients tended to be more sarcastic than funny, they certainly won out over her husband's dry non-humor about the stock market and recollections of studying at Harvard.

20

Even Amelia was quite gregarious (and fortunately she stopped speaking every sentence as a question). She entertained us during the main course about demanding clients who wouldn't look at a house that wasn't painted the right color or didn't have a bidet or those who would only purchase a home with an even-numbered address.

I glossed over my time in the army and told a few stories about working for the BPD. Sunny asked about my future plans and I confessed that I didn't really know what my next move would be. Mindy had to try to ruin the evening by suggesting that Robert get me a job at the resort cleaning guest rooms or in maintenance since I had worked construction on my own house. Robert frowned at Mindy and was spared from replying by Mindy's husband. He looked at me with genuine interest and suggested I could come renovate their outdated house, at which point Mindy nearly had a stroke. A stunned silence fell over the table as Julian bent his head to his phone again and the color rose sharply on Mindy's cheeks.

Chance tried to hide his smile as he started to talk about his former life as a lawyer for a corporate firm in Boston. He told us how he had gotten increasingly disillusioned and longed for a quieter life. He smiled directly at me as he told me that he and his sister were the proud new owners of The Harbor Bar, which they renamed Two Cups, and it would be a combined coffeehouse and wine bar with a small performance stage – if they ever completed renovations.

I stared open-mouthed as I had no idea that Chance Wolf was the person who bought my mother's bar. I had wanted it gone so badly that I barely read the papers the lawyer drew up; I just scrawled my signature on the way to physical therapy one day. I thought now maybe I wouldn't mind hanging out at my mother's old bar but Mindy interrupted this happy thought.

"Let me know when your grand opening will be. I would love to help you coordinate the event and really make a splash. Let everyone see it's no longer the seedy dive bar for lowlifes, degenerates, and criminals it once was."

Silence fell over the table since everyone but Julian knew that my mother had owned the bar and I had spent a lot of my time working and hanging out there. Mindy looked defiantly at everyone then stared directly at me, daring me to contradict her.

Amelia looked harshly at Mindy and seemed ready to admonish her. I swallowed the lump that had just formed in my throat, excused myself, and stalked off to the ladies' room, feeling every eye at the table watch me walk away.

Chapter Six

I waited in the ladies' room until I heard Cal Jr., Harmony High Class of 2000 Class President, welcome the alumni. I slipped out and went to the bar at the back of the dining room with the rest of the lowlifes and degenerates. I hated how Mindy's words could still make me feel worthless. I found a seat where I could see the stage yet stay out of sight of my former tablemates.

I didn't look at the wine menu, just blindly ordered the house pinot grigio, closed my eyes, and sighed inwardly as the first cool sip slid down my throat.

"That wine must be blissful based on the expression on your face."

My eyes flew open and I turned quickly to see Chance standing next to me at the bar. I gave an embarrassed grin and turned back to my drink. Chance pointed to my glass when the bartender came over.

"I'll have one of those, please."

I turned to look at him. "You don't seem like a pinot grigio kind of guy."

"What do you think a guy like me *should* drink?" he asked playfully.

I shrugged. "I don't know." I studied him for a moment. "Perhaps scotch or bourbon, served neat." Or a vodka martini, shaken, not stirred, I thought devilishly.

Chance chuckled. "Well, I have been known to appreciate a good single malt at times but I am opening a wine bar so I have tasted my fair share of wines." He looked speculatively at me and took a deep breath. "Kat, I don't want you to think I agree with those people at the table. Mindy was always a snob and looked down on everyone. Sunny followed the beat of her own drum. Marla Jean, or MJ, I guess, had a rough life

23

which Mindy and her crew always harassed her about, too." He looked down. "Let's face it. High school sucked and nobody enjoyed it, despite their feeble attempts to portray otherwise." He trailed off, then refocused on me. "Anyway, The Harbor was a decent bar. It just needed a facelift. My sister has two passions – coffee and wine, so that's why we decided to change it."

I winced. "No, it was a dive bar and it needed a lot of work. It's just that now that I'm an adult, I hate how people still associate me with a seedy bar and the questionable choices my mother made." I let out a long-suffering sigh. "Before I came back to Harmony, I hadn't stepped in that place for more than fifteen years."

Chance leaned in close and grinned. "It may have been a dive bar but in my experience, those are the best kind." He looked off across the crowd, listening attentively as Amelia now detailed all that was in store for us this weekend. "To be truthful, I had my first beer at The Harbor."

I looked surprised and Chance grinned again. "Yup. Snuck in with my older brother's driver's license when I was only seventeen. I ordered a beer and a shot of Jägermeister." He chuckled. "I was sick as a dog for two days. Never drank that stuff again."

I laughed so hard I snorted and then looked embarrassed. *Ladies don't snort,* I could still hear my grandmother admonishing. Chance leaned close to me. "I sincerely hope to break your fifteen-year streak of not stepping foot in the bar when we open Two Cups."

I smiled at him and released some of the tension I had been holding in my shoulders. "Well, I do appreciate good wine, I just can't always afford it. I spent a few years in Italy when I was in the army and learned everything I could about different varieties and styles." I gave him an appraising look. "I'll be interested to see what you have chosen for your cellar, Mr. Wolf."

24

Chance chuckled. "I do believe I hear a gauntlet being thrown down, Ms. Snow. I developed my nose for wine when I lived in Boston and I feel certain that you'll enjoy my eclectic selection." We grinned stupidly at each other. "Plus, I'll be changing the selections seasonally and will highlight some of the local wineries." He shook his head. "I hated every minute of my ten-year career as a corporate lawyer in Boston. I'm looking forward to a laid-back lifestyle as a bar owner in Harmony."

I looked at him mischievously. "If you lived here…"

He finished my sentence, "…you'd be in Harmony!"

We both laughed so hard about the billboard that still graced the entrance to the town that we received some pointed glares from some of our classmates. As our laughter died down, Chance touched my back and whispered, "I don't think I'm going to make it to the 'Drinks and Dancing' portion of the evening. I'm still wrapping up a few cases for the law firm and need to submit a brief by Monday morning. I want my last case to be over so I can finally enjoy the next phase of my life."

I felt the warmth of his hand on my back through my sweater and was having a difficult time concentrating. "Ok. See you at breakfast tomorrow?"

Chance gave my shoulder a little squeeze and winked as he turned to walk away.

Chapter Seven

The pinot grigio was decent for a house wine and was starting to work its magic. I was definitely feeling more relaxed after my conversation with Chance. I sipped on a second pinot grigio while I watched everyone as the Harmony Alumni Choir sang a few school songs. As I raised the glass to my mouth, I heard, "Put that glass down immediately!" I turned my head slowly, wondering who the voice was talking to.

Marco grinned as he slid onto the barstool next to me. "What swill are you drinking, Kat? That is not one of my wines." He motioned the bartender over. "Armando, we'll have two glasses of the *Rias Baixas Albariño*, please. From my private reserve."

Armando nodded at Marco and went into the back room. He stepped out a moment later with an unopened bottle and went through the proper ritual of opening it. He poured a little for Marco to sip and I watched as Marco inhaled the bouquet and savored the taste with his eyes closed. I had never appreciated Marco's classic Roman appearance until that very moment. Marco's eyes popped open and he waved at Armando to pour the two glasses. "I think you'll like this better than whatever that was," he said, pointing to my near-empty glass. He handed one of the wine glasses over to me.

I looked at Marco curiously. I didn't think he had ever spoken a full sentence to me in high school. I held my glass up to the light to appraise its color, then swirled it gently to test the wine's legs. I nodded appreciatively and then raised the glass to my nose and inhaled deeply. I felt the vapors permeate my soul. Finally, I took a small sip and swirled it around a few times to completely cover my tongue while inhaling a little air to oxygenate the wine. Smiling slightly, I swallowed the sip and then took another, following the same routine. I nodded my head in approval of the wine.

Marco grinned. "I thought you might know your way around a wine glass!"

I looked at him sharply. Was that a remark about my mother being a bar owner? "What do you mean?"

"I can tell by just looking at people if they appreciate a nice glass of wine. You, for instance, are not a boxed wine kind of gal." He looked across the crowd and narrowed his eyes. "Mindy, on the other hand, as pretentious as she is, drinks cheap white zinfandel while reading a romance novel in the tub and fantasizing about the gardener – even though she thinks he should be deported."

I laughed at the mental image then inwardly winced as I recalled my dwindling bank account and the box of wine actually sitting on my counter. Marco continued unaware. "Tell me what you think about the *albariño*."

I took another sip and really concentrated on the flavors. "I'm not good enough to know specific wineries or vintages, but I would say that this wine comes from the Galicia region of Spain. It has notes of lemony citrus and a pine aroma. It tastes bright on the palate with orange and," I inhaled again, "nectarine flavors." I smiled at him as he beamed at me. "I really like it, too."

Marco clapped his hands together in glee. "Splendid. That's what matters most. It's actually from the Casa do Sol Vineyard and rates highly on the *Wine Spectator* rating scale. You should come out to the winery sometime soon. My warehouse of imported wines is there and I think you will really enjoy some of what I want you to taste."

What the hell was happening in my life? First, Chance was all flirty and fun and now Marco is asking me to drink some of his private reserve wine? Damn, I'm speaking in questions again. I shook my head to see if it would help anything make sense. Marco squinted at me, "Are you alright?"

I nodded. "I think so, but I'm not really sure why you're here talking to me. We never even spoke in high school."

Marco looked chagrined. "You're right. I was an absolute jerk in high school. It wasn't until I went away that I realized all I had missed out on in Harmony by somehow believing the bullshit that I was better than everyone else." He turned and took my hand in his. "I'm trying to make amends to anyone I may have offended in the past. Please forgive me if you were one of the many I offended."

He looked so sincere that I could easily forgive him for his attitude back in high school. Hadn't I also done some stupid things back then? He was still holding my hand so I shook his and said playfully. "You're forgiven for whatever you need to be forgiven for, with one request."

He looked at me sincerely, his blue eyes boring deep into mine while his blond hair fell rakishly over his brow. "Name it. What can I do for you?"

"Offer me the friends and family discount on your wines?"

He chuckled and nodded affirmatively. "It's a deal."

We both sipped our wine and listened to another song by the alumni choir. Marco leaned over and whispered, "They really are awful, aren't they?"

I nodded in agreement.

Marco turned around and looked at me again. "So, what were you and Chance chatting about over here during Amelia's agenda review? Between you and Chance having a grand old time and Mindy openly flirting with Bo at the table, Amelia was so peeved, she could barely read her notes." He looked at me appraisingly, "Not that you noticed."

28

I was taken aback again. It seemed like I was really causing a stir at this reunion and it was only the first night. "We were just talking about how he had fixed up my mother's old bar and he apologized for that beast, Mindy Vanderbilt."

Marco winced. "Is Mindy still up to her old tricks? Nasty little minx. She dated me only because she couldn't have Bo."

I looked surprised. "She told you that?"

Marco looked chagrined. "No, but it was obvious. He was all she could talk about all the time. I couldn't stand being around her after two dates." He looked carefully at me. "Are they still being nasty to you after twenty years?"

I nodded. "Mindy more than Amelia. I think Amelia is clueless but she is also trying to make amends. She even upgraded my room here at the resort."

"That's good to hear. She was okay, we just weren't meant to be." He looked over at our table. "She seems happy, I guess, with Bo."

"Don't let her hear you call him that," I warned, adopting a posh accent. "It's Robert now."

"Thanks for the warning." He looked at them again and grinned wickedly. "You know, I'm going to call him Bo all weekend, just to be a jerk."

I laughed. "What happened to making amends?"

He smiled. "Amends are only for people who deserve them." He beckoned to Armando. "Please make sure she drinks exclusively from my reserve wines this weekend."

Armando bobbed his head. "Yes, sir, Señor Milano. I will put a note on her room number so that all the other waitstaff know, too."

Marco slid off his barstool and squeezed my hand. "I need to talk to a vineyard owner in Australia about importing their wines. The damned

29

time difference can be murder on my social life." He started to walk off and then turned around, "I hope you make it to my wine tasting tomorrow. I can use a few educated palates in the audience."

I gave him a thumbs up and promised to be there as I spied Syd and Ricky approaching the bar from the dining room.

Chapter Eight

Syd was practically squealing when she reached my side. She hopped on the barstool next to me and put her chin in her hand as she gazed at me. Ricky draped himself over the back of Syd's barstool and they both looked at me pointedly. I continued to drink my wine, slowly savoring the delicious aroma and taste, ignoring them. Finally, Ricky could no longer contain himself. "Tell us everything!" he demanded.

I looked innocently at the pair. "What are you talking about?"

Syd blew out her breath in exasperation. "You sat at the popular kids' table for dinner, then you had drinks with the two hottest guys from our class. "

"Hey!" Ricky interjected.

Syd shrugged. "Sorry, Ricky. Chance and Marco are both gorgeous and successful and she was sitting here chatting them up like they were old friends." She collapsed back in her chair. "What were you even talking about with them?"

I smiled demurely, "Dinner was mostly okay until Mindy had to ruin it with a crack about degenerates hanging out at my mother's bar and me getting a job as a cleaning lady here at the resort. I came to the bar to get away and Chance came to let me know that he does not agree with those people," I jerked my thumb over my shoulder in the direction of my former table. "He also told me that he and his sister are turning my mother's old bar into a wine and coffee place." I took a breath. "Then, Marco came over and apologized for being a jerk all those years ago in high school and gave me full access to his private wines here at the resort." I tried to look nonchalant. "You know, just a typical Friday evening for me."

We burst out laughing. Syd picked up my wine glass and took a sip. She closed her eyes in appreciation and then looked speculative. "What is this?"

"It's an *albariño* from Spain. I like the citrus notes."

Ricky took a sip also and scrunched up his nose. "I don't like this albino wine. Give me vodka any day!"

I smiled. "It's *albariño*, silly. Fine, you can drink vodka, but we're going to Marco's wine tasting tomorrow afternoon. I can't wait to see what other types of wines he brought for us to taste."

Syd sighed, "Okay, if you want us to go and taste some expensive wines, I guess we can fit it into our busy schedule."

Ricky pouted again. "His wine tasting is at the same time as my presentation. You're both going to blow me off?"

Syd smiled and put an arm around his shoulders. "We'll figure something out so we can do both."

Ricky settled down and we ordered another round of drinks as the Alumni Choir finally finished butchering their songs. Everyone started filing out of the restaurant. Finally, it was just the three of us at the bar and a few small groups scattered about the restaurant making plans for the weekend.

From out of nowhere, we heard, "Will you get your nose out of that damn phone and pay some attention to me?" There was a slight buzzing sound in response.

Syd, Ricky, and I turned to find the source of the outburst. We saw two shadowy figures behind one of the pillars a few feet away.

The angry voice continued, "I don't ask you for very much. Can't you take just one weekend off and act like you still love me?"

The second person could be seen lowering his phone and in an angry voice retorted, "Act like I still love you? Like how you were acting with your old high school boyfriend? Maybe if I had everything handed to me in life and looked like a model then I wouldn't have to work so hard so you could spend every last penny I bring home." He turned abruptly and stalked past us toward the exit. We made eye contact as he went by and he nodded at me as he continued out the door. The other person, obviously Mindy, started crying and ran out the door after Julian.

Syd was the first to recover. "Who was that?"

I looked grimly at them both walking quickly down the hallway. "That was Julian Vanderbilt, Mindy's husband."

Ricky sucked in his breath and whispered, "All is not well in Harmony."

Syd and I nodded in agreement and then Syd jumped off her barstool. "Ty is at the lounge bar waiting for us. I can't be late again." She shimmied unrhythmically. "Let's go dance the night away!" she yelled as she danced toward the door.

Ricky shook his head sadly at me. "When will she learn that she just can't dance?"

I smiled, took his arm, and we followed Syd down the hall toward the Harbor View Lounge.

Chapter Nine

After meeting up with Ty, the four of us ordered drinks and then descended on the dance floor. There were lighted tiles and a rotating disco ball – the Harbor View Lounge did not skimp when it came to nighttime entertainment. We all danced in one large group. I was surprised at how much fun I was having.

After about an hour, my side started to hurt where I got stabbed and I signaled the others that I was going to take a break. Ty and Syd were dancing to "I Will Survive" while Ricky belted out his teenage anthem with a backup chorus of former classmates.

I went to the bar and gulped down a bottle of water. I touched my face and realized how sweaty I was and how much I needed to use the ladies' room. For some reason, there was no ladies' room in the actual lounge. You had to go out and down the hall near the meeting rooms. I bopped my way out of the bar and waved at a few former classmates across the lobby as I started walking a little quicker down the hallway toward the restrooms. Nature was calling very loudly.

As I approached the ladies' room, I saw a rusty smear just before the door. The cop in me was still inquisitive, so I bent down to get a closer look and saw a succession of smears leading down the hall. Putting aside nature's call, I followed the trail of smears to the doors of the Blue Room. By now, I had determined I was following a blood trail and realized I was unarmed and relatively defenseless.

Coach Cal Hobart, Harmony High School's phys ed teacher and Cal Jr.'s father, was coming down the hall, apparently following nature's call as well. He appeared to be quite inebriated but he was also 6' 4" and built like a refrigerator, so I called out to him.

Coach Cal peered down the hall at me and stumbled over to greet me. "Hey, K-Kat," he said, swaying on his feet. "What's up?"

I shrugged. "Not much, Coach. Could you come into the Blue Room with me though? I need to check something for tomorrow's program."

Coach Cal tried to wink at me suggestively but instead closed both eyes. "Sure, K-Kat. I'll check on the *program* with you." He giggled, which was not an attractive sound. "You were always one of my favorite s-students."

I rolled my eyes. Great. Now I'd have to fight off a 300-pound lothario. First things first, though. The blood. I grabbed Coach Cal's arm and steered us in the direction of the Blue Room door. He teetered precariously but managed to stay upright as we entered the room. The room was dark and I stepped to the side to turn on the lights.

As I flipped the light switch, Coach Cal opened his eyes, closed them really quickly, and slurred, "Hey! Turn those off! They're k-killing the m-mood."

The lights didn't kill the mood but something certainly smelled very bad inside. Suddenly, a person, more accurately a person covered with one of the white tablecloths, ran at full speed toward the door. Whoever it was didn't realize how big Coach Cal actually was as they crashed into him, but merely succeeded in spinning him around twice. The fleeing person sidestepped around his twirling body and flew out of the room. I saw the white-shrouded person turn away from the lobby and run toward the service hallway as Coach Cal finally crashed to the floor.

It was all kind of comical and I nearly laughed – until I looked deeper into the room and saw what was causing that smell. MJ Cromwell sprawled on the floor with a few chairs knocked over beside her. In her right hand, she held a wine glass with a trickle of wine dripping out onto

35

the floor. That wasn't what kept my eyes glued to her though. Sticking out of her chest was what looked like a steak knife from the dining room. Her head also had a nasty gash and she was lying in a pool of blood which was growing larger by the second.

Coach Cal spied MJ and all the blood a few moments after me and he screamed high and shrill like a little girl. He turned his face away immediately and vomited on himself and the floor. He quickly regained his breath and tried to stand and run for the door, however, he slid in his own vomit, slammed into the swinging door, and fell halfway through onto the floor, flopping around like a helpless, beached whale. With the amount of blood loss and the color of MJ's skin, I knew she was beyond help, though I bent and checked for a pulse anyway.

I sobered completely as I stared at MJ. I took my mobile phone out of my clutch purse and called 9–1–1. After hanging up with the dispatcher, I called Ty and stepped out of the room to guard the door so that nobody else would "discover" MJ. I managed to get Cal out from between the swinging doors and upright, and then moved him down the hall. He promptly collapsed again on the side of the hall, squeezing his eyes shut, and gasping for air. I leaned against the far wall and waited for the professionals.

Chapter Ten

Ty came striding down the hall less than five minutes later, leading four other police officers who must have just arrived at the resort. He cocked an eyebrow as he stopped in front of me and spied the bloodstains on my clothes. "Are you alright?" he asked with concern.

I nodded my head, the last vestiges of alcohol drifting away. "I'm fine." I looked down. "Not my blood." I pointed to the blood smears in the hallway and took a deep, cleansing breath. "I noticed the marks on the walls as I approached the ladies' room and knew right away they were blood."

I pointed at Cal on the floor. "I enlisted, er, backup and followed the trail down the hallway into the Blue Room. When I turned the lights on, we saw MJ Cromwell on the floor with a steak knife through her heart, a bloody gash on her forehead, chairs knocked over, and a rather large pool of blood." I pointed at Cal. "He vomited and left the room while I checked for a pulse." I shrugged and shook my head.

Ty closed his eyes for a second and then eyed me carefully. "You're okay, though? You've got some blood on your sweater." He motioned two police officers into the Blue Room when more police officers arrived on the scene.

"That must be from when I checked her pulse." I rolled my eyes and looked at Cal again. "Or from when I had to haul him upright to move him down the hallway. I think he got a nosebleed when he fell on the floor."

Ty smirked a little then slid into his professional role. "Did you see anyone else either right before or just after you discovered the body?"

I winced. MJ was now just "a body." I suddenly slapped my hand to my forehead. "I'm such an idiot. I'm sorry, Ty. I completely forgot!"

Ty looked confused. "Forgot what?"

"Right after we entered the room and I turned the lights on, we saw the body lying on the ground and all that blood…" I pointed at Cal. "As he stumbled out and I was trying to process what I saw, someone came running out of the shadows and knocked into Coach Cal as they were trying to get out the door."

"Did you get a good look at the person? See who it was?" Ty quickly demanded.

I shook my head. "Sorry, I didn't. They were running with their head down and had one of the tablecloths wrapped around them, covering their head and body. They were like a white blur racing out of there."

"Which way did they go?"

I pointed further down the hallway. "The person turned right out of the Blue Room and kept running down the service hallway toward the kitchens."

Ty nodded and sent three officers down the hall. They drew their service pistols as they moved down the hallway.

Ty leaned in closer. "Close your eyes, Kat. Take a few deep breaths and try to visualize the white blur."

I complied with Ty's commands and tried to focus on his words. I had done the same things with witnesses as a cop in Boston.

"Any general impressions of this person? Height? Bigger or smaller than Coach Cal?" I could hear a touch of humor as Ty must have looked over at Cal.

I shook my head and shrugged. "Definitely smaller than Coach Cal, but the person was also hunched over and had their hands up and over their head."

"Male or female? Were they wearing perfume or cologne? Did you hear the sound of high heels? Boots?"

I kept my eyes closed for a few minutes and tried hard to visualize the fleeing, tablecloth-clad person. Finally, I shook my head again regretfully. "Sorry, I couldn't tell if they were male or female. I couldn't smell anything over the smell of all that blood and death and vomit." I pointed down at the floor. "The carpet masked the sound of footsteps so I didn't even hear the person approach until they brushed past me and knocked into Coach Cal."

Ty rested a hand on my shoulder. "That's okay, Kat. It's hard to be observant when you've just discovered a dead body. Especially because you knew her."

I stomped my foot in frustration. "I've been trained to be more observant than a regular witness. I was in the military police in the army and then a Boston cop and detective for ten years. I'm supposed to know how to be observant."

Ty sighed and I could tell he was about to launch into the police standard about how stress affects memories when we both heard a commotion at the end of the hall. There was a sea of people crammed into the lobby trying to peer down the hallway to see what was happening. Fortunately, the state police had arrived to help control the scene. Ty shook his head as he walked down the hallway, leaving me with one of the police officers who was guarding the door to the Blue Room. The officer stayed quiet and stoic, awaiting further directions.

A few minutes later, Ty strode back down the hall with a local female officer. "That ruckus is mostly being caused by your two best friends, concerned for your safety. I told them you were okay." He paused for a moment. "I need to collect your clothes and have you write down your statement. It will be better if I get it tonight while it's still fresh in your mind." He gestured at the female officer. "Officer Thermon will take care of you until you can get back up to your room." He looked at me sternly. "I told Syd and Ricky to wait for you in your room, which they should be able to get into within a half hour."

I looked at him inquisitively and Ty sighed. "The state police are conducting a room-to-room search for a white tablecloth, or any tablecloth that doesn't belong, in all the rooms."

An officer returned from down the darkened hallway, shaking his head. He stepped up to Ty and reported, "We didn't find anything, sir, except a few blood drops. Officers Keating and Jablowsky went out the service entrance and are searching the back alley."

Ty sighed. "It appears that our person of interest got away."

I startled. "Person of interest? Don't you mean the killer?"

Ty shook his head. "At this point, we don't know what happened and can't make assumptions. For all we know, the person found MJ just like you did and didn't want to be found standing over a dead body. Maybe they're a just witness, too."

I nodded in agreement. "Yeah, you're right. Sorry, I know better. It's just that I don't like being on this side of an investigation. A witness," I muttered, shaking my head.

Ty chuckled once mirthlessly and looked at me in sympathy. "I know, it sucks," he muttered as he gestured me toward another of the meeting rooms. "Follow Officer Thermon in there and she'll collect your clothes and write out your statement."

I noticed the brown evidence bag and hotel robe and slippers in the police officer's hands. "Okay," I mumbled glumly.

"And Kat," he continued, "I would tell you not to talk about what you found but I know you, Syd and Ricky too well. Just don't talk about it with anybody else." He looked around. "I'd like to close down this whole reunion but the Mayor's here and he's already told me he doesn't want the negative publicity." He grumbled. "As a friend, I want to give you a hug

40

but I know I can't." He held his fist out to me and we fist-bumped. "Consider that a hug."

I shook my head and smiled back at him as I followed Officer Thermon to the empty meeting room. Ty yelled out. "If you remember anything else, don't hesitate to call me day or night!" I waved over my shoulder.

Chapter Eleven

An hour later, I was back in my room with Syd and Ricky. There was a police officer stationed on every floor. The room-to-room search had turned up nothing, and no one was allowed to leave the hotel until the cause of death could be determined.

Ty had stopped in to check on the three of us and mentioned that it was difficult to keep track of everyone. Apparently, the reunion-goers were still engaged in reunion activities, namely attending after-party celebrations in various guest rooms around the resort. Whenever an officer would pop into one of the parties, the celebration would break up and move on to the next room. They had heard snippets of conversation about MJ's death, but nothing really useful.

Ty sipped a cup of coffee from the pot we had ordered from room service and savored the rich flavor. He smiled as he refilled the cup and headed for the door. Ty kissed Syd goodnight on the top of her head and said he'd be out in the mobile command center outside the resort if we needed him for anything. "This coffee sure beats the swill the Auxiliary brews for us in the command center."

Syd and Ricky had been discussing what I had seen in the Blue Room and trying to think up possible motives. They eventually decided that she definitely had been murdered – but without any evidence, they could conclude whatever they wanted.

Syd was also busy on her laptop trying to research the life of MJ Cromwell after she left Harmony. Surprisingly, there wasn't much about her personal life online – mostly publicity shots and press releases.

She shut the laptop with a thud and exclaimed, "I guess if you write steamy romance novels, you don't want people to know too much about you."

Ricky crossed his arms and interrupted, "MJ wrote porn, my dear. Maybe you could call it softcore porn, but it was porn, and bad porn to boot!"

I interjected, "I didn't think it was that bad."

Syd and Ricky pivoted their heads sharply to look at me. Syd's eyes opened wide.

"*You* read MJ's novels?"

"Well, I didn't know that MJ was Marla Jean and I only read one book of the trilogy."

Ricky asked excitedly, "Which one? *Curious in the Kitchen? Curious on the Gridiron? Or Curious at the Resort?"*

I laughed. "I read the first one, *Curious in the Kitchen,* while I was recovering from the stabbing." I blushed. "I had to hide it under my hospital bed mattress whenever I had visitors. One of the male nurses found it one day while he changed my sheets. He chuckled and asked if I enjoyed S&M, too. I couldn't look him in the eye ever again."

Syd and Ricky laughed out loud. Syd blurted out, "Ty and I read all three of them together. We would read a chapter or two before bed and then...eh...try out some of the scenarios she described."

Ricky and I burst out laughing and continued until we could barely catch our breath.

Syd looked indignant. "What? A girl's gotta keep her marriage fresh after three kids and twenty years."

Ricky smiled at her indulgently. "Of course you do, but I don't think I'll ever be able to look at Ty without picturing you two in any of those positions ever again."

We all started giggling as we recalled some of our favorite scenes from the books. The two main characters, Josie and Jasper, met online and Josie's life was changed forever.

"Remember when they started using kitchen utensils to...eh...explore each other? Ricky and I nodded and Syd blushed. "Ty and I almost got caught trying to recreate one of those positions while we were cooking Thanksgiving dinner." She smiled demurely. "It was quite exhilarating."

Ricky looked like he was mentally rereading pages in his mind. "How about when Josie told Jasper about what happened to her in high school? That was disturbing."

Syd agreed. "Yeah, but I think it was just to explain how adventurous Josie always had been and why she had been repressed since high school."

I looked confused. "That must have been in one of the books I didn't read. What happened?"

Ricky took a breath. "In the second book, *Curious on the Gridiron*, Josie tells Jasper about a time in high school that she was partying with three of the guys on the high school football team. She remembered being really out of it, like someone might have drugged her." Ricky looked uncomfortable as he continued, "She woke up and was having sex with one of them while the other two watched and recorded it. And after, they passed the video around to the whole football team." Ricky ducked his head. "She told Jasper that she always felt dirty and betrayed, like people were whispering behind her back for the rest of high school."

Syd said quietly, "In the book, Jasper helped her get over her feelings by taking her back to the high school football field where it happened. They ended up making happier, more adventurous, and consensual memories there."

I let out the breath that I had been holding. "I didn't read that book, just the first one." I looked askance at Syd. "That 'memory' Josie shared," I held up my fingers in air quotes, "sounds a little familiar." I thought for

44

a moment. "I remember hearing about a girl and the football team when we were in high school but I always thought that was just teenage boys bragging about nothing." I looked at Syd and Ricky.

Ricky stared wide-eyed at me. "Do you think the girl was Marla Jean?"

I shook my head. "I really don't think so. Marla Jean was pretty innocent in high school and I never heard any rumors about her at all. She was almost invisible." I pondered for a moment. "I wonder who from our class was close enough friends with her to tell Marla Jean about that event and why she chose to include it in her book? That girl was obviously drugged and raped and had suffered enough."

Syd shrugged. "In the book, Josie was upset at first but it didn't seem to bother her that much."

I scowled, "I still don't get how that's romantic, but to each their own, I guess."

Ricky snapped his fingers. "How about in *Curious at the Resort* when Josie and Jasper join that swingers' group and they all meet up at a swanky resort and room hop all weekend with different partners?"

I was still scowling and looked around. "A resort like this? I think I'm glad I only read that first book. That one definitely seemed to be less sadistic or masochistic or whatever." I threw my hands up in disgust and looked thoughtfully up at the ceiling.

Syd leaned in, "Earth to Kat! What are you thinking about?"

I shook my head and looked at Syd. "Honestly, I'm thinking I've led a dull life romantically but I do not want to participate in any form of S&M or partner swapping to spice it up."

Ricki smiled wickedly, "Maybe this weekend you'll get the chance to spice up your romantic life with one of your two suitors, Chance

45

and Marco, only the two most eligible bachelors from our class. Besides me, of course, but we play for different teams."

I rolled my eyes. "We were just catching up after twenty years. They are not my 'suitors'."

Syd pointed to herself, "They didn't seem to want to catch up with *me*. What about you, Ricky?"

"Not me either and we've *all* been gone for almost all of the past twenty years."

I just shook my head at their antics. "That's one of the problems with this case."

Ricky and Syd groaned and then Ricky feigned falling asleep, "I'm bored! This weekend will NOT be about cases and seriousness."

I frowned at him and continued. "We just don't know details about anyone's life since high school. We don't even know if MJ saw or spoke with anyone from high school. Who would have a motive to kill her?"

Ricky stood up abruptly. "You're right, Kat."

Syd looked at Ricky quizzically. "Why are you agreeing with her?"

I looked at him cautiously. "What am I right about?"

Ricky picked up his phone and accessed Facebook. "We don't know enough about anyone anymore." He started composing a message on the event page. "I think it's time we hosted an after-hours party here in our suite and find out what everyone has been up to the past twenty years."

Syd shook her head and held up her hand. "Ty won't like this idea."

Ricky pointed out, "Ty's not here and perhaps we can learn something that will help his case."

The three of us looked at each other conspiratorially until Syd jumped up and grabbed Ricky's phone. "Okay, let's do it." She hit "Send" and looked over at me still sitting in the hotel robe and slippers. "You go get dressed so people don't get the wrong idea about you." She teased, "Maybe Chance and Marco will make it to our room tonight."

Ricky squealed from where he had gone to stand on the balcony and then twirled around to face us.

Syd and I rushed to his side with worry.

Syd grabbed his arm. "What's the matter?"

"Nothing is the matter and everything is great!" He strutted the length of the balcony and spun to face them. "We need to make *our* party the place to be tonight, so let's order some top-shelf bottles from downstairs and go all out."

Syd and I looked at him in confusion. "Why?"

Ricky grinned maliciously. "Remember, our weekend is on Amelia and Bo. Who wouldn't want to come party in a suite with top-shelf liquor? Everyone will want to be here and we'll find out what people have been up to and, you know, where they were at the time of the murder." He nodded emphatically. "And, we're going to party tonight like it's 1999 – you know, our senior year?"

I chuckled and shook my head as I went back to my room to find something suitable to wear for the rest of the night.

Chapter Twelve

The rest of the night went by quickly. Ten minutes after Syd posted on the Facebook event page, there were ten former classmates sprawled in the suite's living room and out on the balcony. We were all drinking mixed drinks because all of the hotel's wine had been confiscated in case it needed to be tested. MJ had been drinking wine when she collapsed so I guess Ty decided it was better to be safe than have another body on his hands. Even though the cause of death appeared to be the steak knife sticking out of her chest, she may have also been poisoned.

I was enjoying getting reacquainted with some of my former classmates. On the balcony, I could see Syd speaking with Millie Zevo and Stuart O'Laughlin. They had reconnected over Facebook ten years ago and gotten married. Turns out, they both sold life insurance in Hartford, Connecticut and had gone to the University of Connecticut.

Four of Ricky's Robotics Club friends had shown up and were arguing about the benefits of electric versus solar versus diesel-powered robots and kill strength and size versus power output. It was worse than calculus to me so I wandered over and joined Sunny Mason and Ned Anders. They had briefly dated in junior year of high school but broke up when Sunny decided she'd rather date Marco Milano. That was short-lived, as were most of Marco's high school dalliances.

Sunny had attended Le Cordon Bleu in Paris and learned from the best chefs in the world. I had heard rave reviews about her pastries but I didn't want to pack on extra pounds while I still couldn't engage in my usual workout routines. It was hard enough to not eat all day as I sat around the house.

Ned had stayed local and, astonishingly, had become an Episcopalian minister. He received his Master of Divinity at the Episcopal

Divinity School in nearby Cambridge. He was now the Reverend at St. Albans, Harmony's Episcopalian church. His wife had left him for Martin Church, ironically enough, a local used car salesman and they had moved down to Westerly, Rhode Island. Ned seemed a little lonely.

Syd, Sunny, and Ned were having a lively conversation and discussing all the foreign countries each had visited. Syd had taken a grand tour of the European art museums during college but hadn't traveled anywhere since having the kids. Ned had mostly traveled for humanitarian missions but had also enjoyed some exotic vacations. Sunny had apparently worked for a while as a personal baker on a billionaire's yacht and traveled the world, learning new recipes and baking up a storm. She had come back to Harmony when she wanted to settle down and had purchased the local bakery.

As I eased onto the sofa next to Sunny, our door opened and more former classmates joined the party. The conversations around me centered on high school reminiscing and what people were doing now. Sunny was thoroughly entertaining as she talked about all the people she had met and cooked for when she worked on the yacht and their bizarre requests.

Sunny talked about how one A-list actor had requested fish-flavored cupcakes and how a supermodel had requested that her croissants be made only from flour sourced from wheat grown on Mount Everest and butter from Echire, France, one of the most exquisite kinds of butter in the world. She mentioned in passing that, after the success of her first book, MJ had also been a guest on the yacht with a much younger male companion. She wouldn't divulge any more information.

Ned launched into a few stories about altar-boy antics and pranks and it really just felt great relaxing after such a long day. By now, there were about 25 people scattered in small groups around the suite. Juan Morales had brought his guitar and was playing softly in the corner. He had recorded a few albums with some jazz musicians and they toured regularly throughout the United States. I had switched to Grey Goose cosmopolitans since wine was not available, and I was feeling no pain. The door popped open and another small group of former classmates joined the party.

I bristled as I noticed Mindy among the group, especially because she was quite inebriated and needed to be held up by Amelia and Bo. Julian was not with the group and Amelia and Bo dumped Mindy unceremoniously into a nearby chair before making a beeline for the bar. Her tiara was askew and tangled in her now-messy hair. Mindy's unfocused gaze fluttered around and she had a stupid grin on her face – until she locked eyes with me.

Mindy's face contorted into a look of contempt and she slurred loudly, "W-wha arrr we doingk he?" She attempted to push herself out of the chair but collapsed back onto the cushions. "I don wanna be n-n-nearrr herrrrr," she stuttered out.

People glanced at her and moved away. I held back every instinct to be spiteful and grabbed a bottle of water from the bar for her instead. I leaned close to Mindy and whispered in her ear, "It's okay, Mindy. Being poor isn't catchy," and smiled as I walked away, leaving Mindy to sputter behind me. Even Amelia looked at Mindy disdainfully.

I had a momentary twinge of sympathy for Mindy but then remembered all the hurtful, mean, and cruel things she had done and said to me in high school – and tonight! – and pushed the sympathy away. I turned to talk to the group gathered around Juan – Syd, Bo, and Bradley and Shannon Craft. Bradley was mayor of Harmony; everyone called him Mayor Brad. Shannon was a stay-at-home mom, working on writing a book in her spare time. Brad was in our class but Shannon was about six years younger than us. I used to babysit her and knew her fairly well.

The years had not been kind to Brad and he was both obese and bald – not the cool kind of bald where a man chooses to shave his head, but the kind where his hair has just kind of disappeared, leaving a fringe around his ears and the base of his skull. Shannon was laser-focused on Brad like he was the most attractive and captivating man at the party. He certainly was not.

Shannon had plans for Mayor Brad. I listened in as Shannon told Juan that she saw Brad becoming mayor as only the first step in a long political career. Brad had graduated from Harvard Business School and then took over his family's restaurant supply business. He focused the business on larger, commercial accounts and ended up becoming the number-one premium restaurant cutlery supplier on the East Coast. Shannon was planning his first state representative campaign and had emphasized that once he was elected into state office, then he could set his sights on Congress or governor, she hadn't decided which yet. She looked coyly around and waved her hand dismissively. "I don't want him to run for President. The stress of that job is just too much on the whole family."

I asked, in all seriousness, "What are his positions on the major issues?"

Shannon looked at me as if I had asked if the moon was made out of Swiss cheese. "His positions are whatever the party wants his positions to be, Kat. That's how people get elected these days."

Meanwhile, Mayor Brad's conversation with Syd and Bo currently seemed to be centered around school budgets and how arts programs would have to be cut. Syd was passionately arguing how funding for the arts was necessary for young minds to develop and thrive. Mayor Brad just kept shaking his head in disagreement.

I decided I was bored and, as I turned to slip away, walked right into Chance, knocking us both a little off-balance. Chance's hands came up to my arms to steady me and I felt a little flutter run through my system.

Chance smiled lazily, "Where are you off to so quickly?"

I nodded over my shoulder at the group that was still arguing about politics. "I am in too good of a mood right now to get into a debate about school budgets." I glanced out onto the empty balcony. "I think I'll get some air."

"Good idea," he agreed and put his hand on my back as he steered me to the balcony. I caught Ricky's eye from across the room and he waggled his eyebrows at me suggestively. I snickered at Ricky's exaggerated facial expression and stumbled a little over the threshold to the balcony.

Chance chuckled as he once again kept me upright and I grinned sheepishly. "I guess I shouldn't mix wine with vodka." Chance ducked back inside and I thought for a moment that he had deserted me until he came back with two icy bottles of water.

"I should hydrate also," he remarked as he opened a bottle and handed it to me before opening the second and taking a big gulp. I watched as water droplets dripped onto his shirt.

"Did you finish your brief?"

Chance sighed. "Not quite. There are a few loose ends and citations I still need to research before it's complete. I needed a break though, and this after-hours popped up at just the right moment."

I was about to ask Chance more about his plans for the wine bar when Marco popped his head out of the balcony door.

"Is this a private party or can anyone join?"

Chance sighed exaggeratedly. "Come on out, Marco. It's not like we could stop you if we wanted to anyway."

52

Marco winked at me and stepped out onto the balcony with a glass of wine.

I looked at him accusingly. "What are you drinking?"

Marco shrugged. "My *albariño*, of course."

I narrowed my eyes. "The police confiscated all the wine in the hotel."

Marco took a long swallow and waved his hand dismissively. "I had one of my staff at the winery bring me a fresh bottle." He raised his glass. "Wine is life, my dear. Well, it's *my* life."

I opened my mouth to reply when we suddenly heard loud pounding at the suite door.

I gritted my teeth and started moving toward the door. I could see Syd and Ricky on their way as well. We had just entered the small foyer when the door slammed open and Ty and four police officers came charging through the door. Ty took a long look at us and the party going on behind us. I watched the color rise in his cheeks as that little vein on his right temple began to throb menacingly.

"What do you think you are doing?" He addressed Syd but I knew it was meant for all three of us.

Syd stared mutely up at Ty. Ricky suddenly found the floor very interesting. I couldn't find the words to explain – a first in my life.

Syd took a deep breath and retorted defiantly, "We decided to host an after-hours party so we could get reacquainted with *our* high school friends."

By this time, the whole party had quieted down and was staring toward the door. Ty was sputtering in exasperation. "You wanted to get *reacquainted?*" He looked at the three of us. "Did it occur to any of you that one of your high school *friends* may have killed Marla Jean Cromwell?"

53

Ricky tried to deflect Ty's anger. "We were all just hanging out, having drinks, and catching up."

Ty took a deep, measured breath. "You are all aware that Marla Jean was killed while 'drinking and hanging out'" (Ty added air quotes for emphasis) "probably with one of her high school friends?" He took a deep breath. "I don't expect you two," he pointed a finger at Syd and Ricky, "to know better, but Kat," now he skewered me with his gaze, "you were a cop. A homicide detective. *You* should have been the voice of reason."

I looked at the nearly thirty people scattered around the room, all staring at me. I looked at Ty apologetically and whispered, "You're right. I'm sorry."

Ty didn't know what to do with an apology. He had expected an argument, or at least an excuse. He growled in frustration and threw his hands in the air. "We can talk about this later." He turned to the room. "Party's over, everyone. It's late and you all have a full day tomorrow." Everyone started heading for the door. Ty groaned. "Please check in with one of the officers as you leave and leave your drinks here, please." He turned to his officers and murmured, "Make sure you write down everyone's name and room number, or address if they're not staying at the hotel."

The four officers stepped into the hallway and began gathering information from each guest as they left. Amelia and Bo had Mindy with them again but she was now completely passed out. Ty's ire wasn't completely dissipated yet and he watched incredulously as they shuffled Mindy out the door. He turned to the three of us again.

"How could you let Mindy get so inebriated?" he demanded.

Syd held up her hand. "That's not on us. She showed up here inebriated. She didn't even have one drink here. I saw Kat give her a bottle of water. That's it."

54

Ty scrubbed his face with his hands and muttered through them, "Okay, okay. Sorry."

He looked over at Syd and back at the nearly empty room and muttered impatiently, "I'm going to leave now and you better not have any more bone-headed ideas." He leveled a steady gaze at each of us. "I know you. I'm sure you were trying to come up with clues to help me solve Marla Jean's murder."

The three of us looked around. I was about to reply when Syd elbowed me in the side to shut me up. "Okay, dear." She looked at me and Ricky. "We won't have any more bone-headed ideas."

Ty eyed us suspiciously. "I have half a mind to order you three to check out and go home but at least I know where you are if you're in the hotel."

I felt my anger rise and bristled. "You are not the boss of me, Ty Randall." I looked pointedly at Syd and then back at Ty. "You're not *my* husband either so you can forget all that 'ordering me around' swagger."

Ty's shoulders sagged. "I didn't mean it like that, Kat. I'm just exhausted and," he looked around to see if anyone was close, "we don't have any leads yet." He sighed. "I'm worried the state police will take over and relegate the Harmony Police Department to babysitting duties for the reunion guests."

I sighed and Syd rushed into his arms. "You'll solve the case, sweetie. You're the smartest man I know," I looked sidelong at Ricky who smartly, for once, stayed quiet. "Well, common-sense smart. Nobody is as smart as Ricky."

Ty wrapped an arm around Syd and looked over her head at Ricky who was blushing a little bit. "I hope so." He kissed the top of her head and looked pointedly at me. "Now, I'm not telling you what to do but if I could choose anything to do right now, it would be to go to bed."

I looked at the mess in the room with all the glasses and bottles strewn about and felt all my energy drain away. "This will all be here in the morning. I could use a good night's sleep."

Ty smiled tiredly and left. As I stepped forward to close the door, Chance poked his head back in.

"See you at breakfast?" he grinned mischievously.

I smiled. "Of course."

Chapter Thirteen

The next morning appeared bright and sunny as I slowly opened one eye. For some reason, I seemed to be lying face down on a cloud. A soft, fluffy cloud. No, wait! That couldn't be right. I opened my other eye, then immediately closed both as the sunlight streaming through the windows made me feel nauseated. Damn! Why did I mix wine and vodka last night? I felt like death warmed over. Maybe I should just roll over and go back to sleep for a few hours…

I sat up abruptly as memories of last night washed over me. The nausea would just not stop. Death? Right, Marla Jean, MJ, had been killed last night. No more famous writing career, movie deals, or jet-set vacations on swanky yachts for her. My head was pounding as I pushed myself off the cloud – bed – and shuffled to the bathroom, trying to shield my eyes from the sunlight. I told myself I'd feel better if I brushed my teeth.

A few minutes later, I realized I had lied to myself. I still felt horrible. I reached into my toiletry bag and carefully rooted around for the Advil. That should help. And a Coke. I wanted a Coke. I walked carefully to the door of my bedroom and opened it cautiously. Ricky and Syd were sitting on the balcony laughing and drinking what looked to be mimosas. I gagged a little at the thought of more alcohol in my body right now. I snagged a bottle of Coke from the mini-bar – who cared if it would cost me, or the Beauregards, three dollars – and swallowed the three Advil I had found in my bag.

Syd saw me and bounced out of her chair to help me to the balcony, snickering sadistically at my condition.

"How come you two aren't hungover?" I inquired suspiciously.

"We stopped drinking early and we didn't mix our alcohols," Ricky quipped bluntly as he cocked his head at me in a mean girl pose.

I pulled a face at him and sank slowly into one of the chairs. I reached over for a croissant and started to pull it apart while Syd poured me a cup of coffee.

I waved her away. "I don't drink coffee. Never have. Never will."

Syd smiled knowingly. "It's really the best hangover cure, even if you're not a regular coffee drinker."

I slowly brought the cup to my mouth, inhaled, and took a tiny sip. I shuddered and put the cup down, the bile rising once again. "Nope. You are never going to convert me to being a coffee drinker."

Syd and Ricky laughed as I took another sip of my Coke. We looked back into the room and saw all the empty bottles and cups. I looked back at them. "What say we leave this mess and let housekeeping take care of it? We can leave them a HUGE tip when we check out."

Ricky clapped his hands in delight, causing my head to reverberate as if a gong had been struck nearby. "That's a spectacular idea, Kat." He grabbed up the reunion agenda. "What do we want to do first?"

Syd smiled slyly. "Well, Kat has a date if she can get dressed and make it down to breakfast."

I shook my head slowly in confusion. "I don't have a date. What are you…" I suddenly remembered telling Chance twice last night that I would meet him at breakfast. I took another sip of Coke then grabbed Syd's mimosa and tossed it back.

Ricky gasped and his eyes nearly popped out of his head. "What are you doing?"

I grimaced and poured myself another mimosa. "I need some 'hair of the dog' to cure this hangover!"

"Sounds like a plan. We'll join you," Ricky chuckled as he grabbed the orange juice and prosecco.

58

Syd, Ricky, and I made it down to the Breakfast Nook at 8:50. I spied Chance sitting with Marco, Amelia, and Bo near the windows. Chance waved us over and a waiter rushed to slide another table on the end so we would have enough room. We quickly ordered more croissants, coffee, and mimosas. Chance cocked an eyebrow at me.

I ignored his look but Syd said sweetly, "This is a mini-vacation and if we want to day drink, Chance Wolf, we do not need your approval."

Chance laughed and ordered mimosas for the whole table. "No disapproval, Syd. All this drinking bodes well for my bar."

I was about to take a drink of the pretty cocktail when I froze, the glass inches from my mouth.

Ricky leaned in and whispered, "What's the matter?"

"Prosecco is wine. I thought the police confiscated all the wine last night because they thought it may have been poisoned?" I looked over at Marco.

Marco smiled cockily. "I guess that's the benefit of having a friend in the wine business." He looked around cockily. "I had my staff restock the resort this morning before breakfast so there won't be any interruptions to our reunion festivities." He picked up a bottle. "All the bottles that came today are marked with a sticker from Milano Importers so we know they're safe."

I smiled at Marco. "That was very kind of you, Marco." I could feel my hangover fading into a not-so-distant memory.

"I know," he replied cheerfully.

Amelia cleared her throat. "You need to eat quickly if you are going to seaside yoga. I don't think I'll make it as I want to add something to the Memoriam for Marla...MJ."

Marco stage whispered, "Inconvenient of her to die with such short notice."

59

Amelia gave Marco a look of exasperation while Bo quickly looked away, trying not to smile. "B...Robert. Let's go. I want to be sure everything is perfect for the memorial."

Bo stood up but then bent down next to me. "I hope you are enjoying the suite. I'm so glad you three were able to make it to the reunion. Amelia would never say anything but she was worried that you, Syd, and Ricky wouldn't attend."

I started and looked at him in confusion. "Amelia was worried *we* wouldn't come to the reunion? That's odd."

Bo sighed and straightened up, addressing the table. "She feels really bad about how she treated you in high school, especially after we heard about what happened to you in Boston. She's kind of turned over a new leaf. Since we started attending church again, you know, when Reverend Anders – Ned – took over, she has been dedicated to be more positive and wants to atone for the sins of her past." He looked at me as she beckoned to him from the doorway. "She's very stressed about this weekend and now with the murder..." He looked pained. "She's truly quite different person now than in high school." He rested a hand on my shoulder. "Our faith has changed us both, for the better. Please give her a chance."

I sat there stunned as Bo caught up with Amelia and they left to review the plans for the memorial event.

Marco, never one to let a moment go by unremarked, said, "Well, chalk one up for religion," and made a tally mark in the air. We all rolled our eyes at him.

Ricky, Syd, and I knew we wouldn't have time to eat *and* go to yoga – and I didn't particularly want to go to yoga, so we lingered over breakfast instead. Chance and Marco were comparing cars and each claimed theirs was better. They decided to go inspect each car in person

60

and were bickering as they walked away. I shook my head. Sometimes boys just do not grow up.

Syd elbowed me and nodded toward the door. I swiveled my head and watched as Julian and Mindy came in. Mindy looked even worse than I had felt that morning. Her hair was stringy and her face was a sickly green color. She had on dark glasses and sank slowly into the closest chair. I heard her order coffee and dry toast. Her husband, Julian, meanwhile, had not raised his head from his phone. He just ordered coffee and kept typing.

Mindy looked over at our table and frowned, then pointedly turned her back on us. She reached over and batted her husband's phone down. "You know the deal. No gadgets at breakfast."

Julian deflated and sighed. "Yes, dear."

The two sat there, staring at each other in silence while Ricky, Syd, and I finished our breakfast. As we walked by Mindy's table a few minutes later, I heard Julian clicking away on his phone held low in his lap and hidden by the tablecloth. It appeared that Mindy had fallen asleep, her head nestled in the cushions of the wingback chair.

Chapter Fourteen

When the Breakfast Nook closed, we moved to sit on the back patio, overlooking the pool. As the day slowly warmed, there was a handful of people stretching and groaning on the yoga platform near the pool. From my perspective, and after quite a few mimosas, it was quite comical to watch. Ricky pulled out the reunion agenda and exclaimed excitedly, "Let's go do the obstacle course!"

Syd and I groaned and Syd shook her head. "I think I'm going to head to the spa and get a relaxing massage." She stretched and looked around. "Even though the girls are older now, I still spend so much time running around and taking care of everyone else. I need a break."

Ricky turned to me with a big smile. "Guess it's just you and me then, Kat."

I firmly shook my head. I had spotted Sunny over by the pool and wanted to chat with her some more.

Ricky stomped his foot. "Come on! I can't do it on my own. I need a partner!'

Marco came out from the lounge just in time to hear Ricky. "Hey! I wanted to do that obstacle course, too, and I don't have a partner. Chance had to go do some boring work and he'd be deadweight anyway." He eyed Ricky. "With your brains and my brawn, Riku," he pantomimed flexing his muscles, "we can't lose. Plus," he leaned in conspiratorially, "I heard the prizes are incredible."

Ricky jumped up. "You're on – and nobody calls me Riku except my parents!"

They fist-bumped and walked away without a backward glance at us. Syd looked at me and started snickering, "I think you just lost one of your suitors, Kat."

I watched their retreating backs and then turned to Syd. "Really? I don't get that vibe from Marco at all," I replied doubtfully.

Syd shrugged. "It's not always so overt anymore." She smiled affectionately at me, "Ricky needs a new boyfriend. That last one was such a jerk and broke his heart, and anyway, you don't need two."

"I don't even have one, Syd, but I'm just saying I don't see it."

"We'll see. You just don't want to lose such a hot guy to Ricky."

I laughed. "Maybe that's it."

Syd got up and stretched her arms languorously over her head. "I'm off to the spa for some pampering." She leaned over and looked at the agenda that Ricky had left behind. "I'll meet you at 12:30 for the luncheon."

"You're not going to the memorial?"

Syd shook her head. "This weekend was supposed to be about happiness and fun. I plan on getting as many services at the spa as possible before lunch. And...," she eyed me and shook her head, trailing off.

"What?"

She huffed. "I know you're not going to listen to Ty's directions. You're going to investigate MJ's murder."

I stared open-mouthed at her. "What?"

"Don't be coy with me, Kat Snow. I've known you forever." She cracked a smile. "Just don't let Ty find out what you're doing." Then she flounced into the hotel, leaving me chuckling to myself.

I stood up and stretched as well. Late night drinking and little sleep did not agree with my body and I could feel my scars throbbing. I took a slow, deep breath as my physical therapist had taught me and slowly let it out. I visualized the tension and fatigue leaving my body. Not for the first time, I thought how getting older was no fun at all.

Sunny was sitting by herself in a lounge chair by the pool, wearing a skimpy orange bikini and sporting a nice tan. I rubbed my scar from the stabbing and sighed. I felt frumpy in my comfortable shorts and a tank top as I sat next to Sunny.

"How do you stay so thin with all that delicious food you cook?" I asked.

Sunny smiled slyly. "I'll tell you my secret. I only take one bite when I cook something fattening. That way, I don't feel like I'm depriving myself but I don't overindulge. I know there's going to be something equally as delicious the next day so it's not that hard to stay strict with myself." She shrugged. "It's the only way I could survive without binging and purging." She looked off at the harbor. "I tried that for a while and that certainly didn't work."

I was astonished. "I'm sorry. I didn't mean to pry."

Sunny grinned. "That's okay. Sometimes confession is good for the soul." She looked around. "Where are your friends?"

I shook my head. "Ricky went to do that obstacle course with Marco and Syd wanted a spa treatment."

"They left you to solve MJ's murder on your own?"

I threw up my hands in the air. "Why does everyone think I'm trying to solve this murder?"

"You were always curious, Kat. It's your nature. That's why I liked being your partner in chemistry." She leaned back and put her sunglasses on. "I was not surprised at all that you became a detective."

I smiled and gave in. "Okay, so, do you know anything about MJ since she left Harmony? At dinner, you said she once sailed on the yacht where you were the chef."

Sunny frowned. "Yeah, that was about ten years ago, after the first book became so popular and they were talking about making it into a

64

movie." She reached for her drink, a bright red smoothie, and took a long draw from the straw. "After those drinks last night, I can really use these antioxidants." I nodded knowingly.

"She made sure I knew to call her MJ and not Marla Jean. She had fixed her hair and teeth and definitely had some work done, if you know what I mean." Sunny held her hands up to her chest and then pulled them away, miming a large chest size.

"Oh," I said. "I wondered. She certainly didn't have those in high school."

"Right?" Sunny smirked. "She also didn't have the much younger, hot boyfriend."

I leaned in. "Was he someone famous? Someone I might know?"

Sunny shook her head. "No, but we do know his older sister. He was from Harmony."

"Really? Who was he? Someone we went to school with?"

Sunny shook her head. "I really shouldn't say. I promised MJ, and then, after what happened to him…"

My thoughts were spinning in my head as I tried to formulate my next question. Sunny didn't wait for me and continued on with her story. "We actually spent a lot of time together on that trip. I think she was happy to see someone she knew and could just be her old self with." She took another sip of her smoothie. "She would come and hang out with me while I cooked and she even brought some wine down to drink with me in my quarters." Sunny sounded wistful. "We talked about high school and how horrible it had been for both of us."

I stared at her. High school was horrible for Sunny the cheerleader? How could that be? It had all seemed so perfect – she had always looked so perfect. I guess that's how things appear from the outside.

Sunny continued, "I felt really close to her that week. Closer than I had to anyone in a long time. We gossiped and told each other things…well, I told her things I had never told anyone."

I was watching Sunny intently and saw the heartache in her eyes. She abruptly sat up and looked at her watch as she swiped absently at her eyes. She forced a cheery tone. "Look at the time! I really need to go if I want to change for the memorial." She stood up and draped a sarong around her tanned, lithe body. "Ciao, Kat. See you later!"

Chapter Fifteen

I didn't know who I should speak to next. I laid back on the chaise lounge and enjoyed the warmth of the sun on my body. I must have drifted off because I woke up abruptly when Ricky and Marco plopped down on the chair next to me.

"Hey, Kat," Ricky began excitedly. "Look at what we I won!"

I blinked my eyes and stretched as I sat up. I could feel that headache sneaking back in. Marco beckoned to the waiter as Ricky flashed an envelope in front of me.

"What did you win?"

Ricky opened the envelope and pulled out two passes. "We won a membership for two at The Mercury."

I shrugged. "At the what?"

Ricky wagged his finger in my face. "The Mercury— the elite fitness gym in town owned by Cal Mercury Jr., Coach Cal's son." I must have still looked blank, because he shook his head. "You don't get it, Kat. The Mercury is exclusive. There is a waiting list to join. I've had my name on the list since I moved back to Harmony. It's got all the best equipment—even new stuff that's in beta testing and their trainers have all worked with Olympic athletes."

"Okay, then." I tried to look suitably impressed. "I hope you both enjoy it," I stretched, trying to relieve the pain in my side.

"Oh, we will—right, Marco?"

Marco handed me a glass of sparkling wine. "I don't need it, sport. I have a membership already."

Ricky then looked at me expectantly.

I shook my head vehemently. "No! No! No! I am not joining some posh gym with you, Ricky. I like working out in my home gym."

Ricky looked pleadingly at me. "You know that Syd will NEVER go to the gym with me, Kat. Please? And Ty works out with his cop buddies at the boxing gym on Valley Street," He looked at me with such puppy dog eyes that I felt myself nodding even though I was still definitely thinking no.

"Yay!" Ricky jumped up and started dancing around, then threw his arms around me. I groaned as he squeezed my throbbing side. "This is going to be so much fun. I can't wait to try out the lap pool and I heard there's even some of Sebastien Lagree's Supraformers and Megaformers."

Was Ricky speaking Japanese? I had never heard those words before. "Wait, a Supra...what?"

"It is the latest in exclusive, high-tech gym equipment. Cal Jr. worked as a fitness trainer in Los Angeles for a bunch of celebrities. He became friends with Sebastien Lagree and was able to get some of his exclusive machines for The Mercury." Ricky was nearly drooling over the free membership vouchers.

Marco chuckled at Ricky's glee and my terror-stricken face. "Relax, Kat. It's a free membership. If you hate it, you don't have to go."

Ricky looked at me in horror and punched Marco hard on the arm. "Don't even suggest that, you Neanderthal."

Marco winked at Ricky. "We both know that Kat is not a quitter. Right, Kat?"

I gulped down my sparkling wine. "There's a first time for everything." I stood up. "Now, let's go pay our respects to our departed classmates."

Ricky tucked the envelope into the pocket of his cargo shorts and Marco handed us each another glass of sparkling wine—he seemed to have a never-ending supply? The three of us wandered back to the hotel, past some cops who were not doing such a great job of blending in. They were obviously on hand to watch for suspicious behavior and make sure everyone was safe.

Chapter Sixteen

Only two of our classmates had died—well, three now, including MJ. Willa Jenkins had breast cancer that metastasized and left her husband with two young children to raise on his own. Her husband, Benton, had created a beautiful poster, a collage of pictures of their too-short life together. He gave a brief but moving speech about Willa and talked about how the cancer had moved quickly through her body. Willa and I had played volleyball together in high school, but we had lost touch after graduation and I was sad that I would never get a chance to reconnect with her.

Wallace Humphreys, on the other hand, had been the class jerk. He wasn't very bright so he overcompensated by being mean to everyone. Girls were scared of him because if you caught his eye, he'd creepily stalk you until he found someone else to obsess over. Guys didn't like him because he was always trying to pick a fight to prove he was a tough guy. I had always felt a little bad for him because I knew he had a rotten home life. His parents were nightly regulars at my mother's bar, leaving Wallace in charge of his two little brothers. I felt really bad for them, but I still didn't want to be his friend.

The apple didn't fall far from the tree— Wallace turned into an alcoholic who couldn't hold down a job after high school. He was fired from the local Meineke for being drunk on the job and ended up fixing cars for anyone who asked— when he was sober. Never married, he was arrested numerous times for DUI, and finally ended up driving off the side of the road into a large oak tree one night. One of his brothers had brought a few pictures, and he tried not to make Wallace sound pathetic, but it's kind of hard to make a cheerful eulogy about a life that futile.

I had to give Amelia credit. She had only about 12 hours but still managed to pull together a moving memorial for MJ. There were pictures of her from high school, although I couldn't fathom where they had come from. I had always felt that MJ and I had been a bit invisible during high school. I think the only picture of me in the yearbook was my class photo. There were also publicity shots of MJ promoting her books, attending movie premieres, and celebrating on various red carpets, which must have been pulled off the web. Since there were no family or close friends there to eulogize MJ, Amelia read some biographical information from her publisher and tweets from people MJ knew in Hollywood who posted when her murder hit the news earlier that day.

It was a nice memorial until Mindy stood up and strode to the front of the room. Her sneer telegraphed that she was not about to say something nice— and she didn't disappoint. "MJ Cromwell was a phony and a fake. Her *new* life was a façade to cover up the insignificant person she was in high school and always would be." She looked meanly out at her fellow classmates. "I mean, really, who here even knew her? I bet none of you knew what kind of person she became— a user and a taker and...and...a killer!"

Every single person at the memorial gasped at Mindy's words. Amelia and Bo were tight-lipped as they quickly mounted the small stage and none-too-gently escorted Mindy off and out the door. A few people followed them out. I couldn't hear what they were saying but there were definitely angry words being exchanged. I nudged Ricky and Marco as everyone stood and then heard anxious whispers wondering what Mindy could have meant.

"Let's go look at those photos," I pointed discreetly at the poster board Amelia had created for MJ. Marco was sipping a glass of wine— again? Where did he keep getting them? – and shrugged his shoulders in

71

agreement. I took the glass out of his hand and sipped from it. "You could have at least gotten me a glass, too," I reprimanded as my eyes closed in pleasure. I looked at Marco questioningly. "A Napa Valley Cabernet Sauvignon?"

He smiled and nodded approvingly. "Do you know which vineyard?"

I shook my head. "Of course not. I'm not that much of an oenophile."

"Not yet," Marco teased. "It's from the Dakota Sky Vineyard, 2017 vintage." He took the glass back and raised three fingers to the waiter hovering in the back. The waiter nodded and slipped out the service entrance, returning a minute later with three glasses of the crimson liquid. Marco exchanged his empty glass for a full one, then handed one to me. He nudged Ricky, who was examining MJ's photo memorial, to take the last.

I smiled. "I guess the waitstaff all know you here?" I savored my next sip of wine. "This really is quite good."

Marco half-bowed. "I'm glad I can be of service."

We both turned to look at the pictures, and I noticed that Ricky was closely examining one photo in particular.

"What's up, Ricky?" I inquired.

He pointed at one of the photos. "I think we know the guy here with MJ at the premiere of one of her movies, *Curious on the Gridiron.* I'm pretty sure it was that film because it was directed by Clinton Foxworth and he's standing next to MJ."

I would never understand how Ricky could remember such worthless trivia.

Marco and I crowded in to look at the picture.

"Which guy do you think we know?" I asked.

Ricky sighed in exasperation. "The tall, skinny guy standing on her other side? Isn't he from Harmony?"

Marco was staring hard at the picture. "He looks vaguely familiar, but I can't quite place him."

I bent and squinted at the picture, then stood up quickly when I realized who it was, my eyes opening wide.

Ricky and Marco both turned, waiting for me to share the news. Ricky couldn't contain himself any longer and burst out, "Don't keep it to yourself, Kat, tell us!"

I was slowly shaking my head. "I probably wouldn't recognize him at all except I used to babysit him when he was a toddler. That's Mindy's little brother, Xavier. He was probably only 9 or 10 when we all moved away from Harmony."

Juan had provided music for the memorial and had apparently been eavesdropping on us while he packed up his guitar. He joined us by the poster and asked, "Are you talking about MJ and Xavier Sherwood?"

Ricky, Marco, and I all turned to stare at Juan. "Do you know why he's in this photo?" I asked.

"They were a couple."

My eyes widened as I started doing the math in my head. "He's at least 11 years younger than us!"

Juan shrugged. "Yeah, well... Xavier moved out to LA right after he graduated high school, with dreams of becoming a star. Mindy told him to contact me to see if I could hook him up with any acting gigs but," he shrugged, "I only know musicians." He glanced back at the picture of MJ and Xavier. "So, Mindy suggested he look up MJ. Two weeks after he called me, I ran into the two of them together at some club. He wasn't even old enough to drink, but there he was, attending to MJ's every desire and she was definitely enjoying the attention."

Ricky looked at the picture speculatively. "Did she get him a part in one of her movies?"

Juan shook his head. "Nah, he gave up the acting dream when he hooked up with MJ. She required 24/7 obedience and promised him a role in her next film if he quit going to auditions." He shook his head sadly. "She strung him along for less than a year, and then she dumped him for her next flavor of the month. He was devastated."

Ricky let out a low whistle. "That's pretty cold." Ricky looked at the picture again. "He would have been better off if he had gotten in touch with Cal Jr. Didn't he have a lot of celebrity clients? Maybe he could have helped Xavier get his foot in the door with a small role."

I looked across the room to where Cal Jr. was holding court, laughing and joking with some of his old friends. "Do you think he would have helped Xavier?"

Juan shrugged. "I don't know. Probably not, after what happened with him and MJ."

Ricky eagerly leaned in form more gossip. "What happened with Cal and MJ?"

"When MJ's first book started becoming really popular, her publisher decided she needed a makeover – a look that would project a more sexual being. He sent her to a surgeon and hired Cal Jr. to help her get into peak physical shape." He sighed. "Did you know Cal Jr. and I drove out to LA together after high school? He went to UCLA on a football scholarship and I went to their school of music."

I stared at Juan. "I never even knew you two were friends in high school."

Juan chuckled. "We were neighbors and had known each other forever. We weren't friends exactly, and never hung out in the same social circles, but it was nice to know someone when I was so far from home.

74

We were even roommates for a little while after graduation. We stayed in touch and would meet for a drink occasionally."

Juan looked at the pictures of MJ. "It was about three years after we graduated that MJ's publisher contacted Cal. Cal was shocked when she showed up for her first training session and he realized that he knew her." He looked across at Cal. "I remember him telling me over drinks about how hard MJ was working and how she had really transformed herself. He said that he was falling for her, and then looked embarrassed that he was attracted to Marla Jean Cromwell."

Ricky was engrossed in Juan's story. "What happened? Did they break up over Xavier?"

Juan shook his head. "They dated and lived together for about a year, I guess. The next time I saw Cal I asked about MJ and he said he had no idea what she was up to or who she was with. He made it seem like he had dumped her, but I knew him well enough to know that he had gotten dumped and was pretty upset about it still. MJ wasn't satisfied with any guy for long."

I took a deep breath and let it out slowly. "I can't believe how much MJ changed from high school. She was always so sweet and nice."

Marco was still peering at the photos and tapped on the picture of Xavier. "Where is this guy now?"

Juan looked down at the floor and scuffed his feet. "Xavier was completely heartbroken when MJ broke it off with him. He had never had a serious girlfriend before and thought it would last forever. He had also gotten hooked on drugs while with MJ." He looked up at me with a tear glistening in his eye. "I heard he killed himself a few months later with a shotgun."

The three of us winced at this news. "No wonder Mindy called MJ a killer!" I felt both shocked and numb. "How do you know so much about all this, Juan?"

Juan sighed. "Because Mindy called me up and chewed me out for not helping her baby brother. She told me that he killed himself and that it was my fault. She said that if I had helped him find an acting gig, he never would have called MJ and ended up having his heart broken and addicted to drugs." Juan wiped a tear from his eye and looked away. "Maybe she was right, but there really was nothing I could do."

Marco threw an arm around Juan's shoulders and gave him a side hug. "You can't blame yourself, man. It's not on you. Mindy had no right to expect you to find her brother a job or to blame you for anything." He surreptitiously swiped at his eyes as well.

Ricky nodded and joined in on the man hug. "He's right, Juan. Not your fault, man."

I felt out of place with this show of bro solidarity. I looked away, out the window down toward the harbor. I wondered how many more secrets Harmony held and had an uneasy feeling that more would come to light before the end of the reunion.

Chapter Seventeen

Ricky, Marco, and I rushed over to the Harbor Restaurant Patio for the "Recognition Luncheon" to make sure we could all sit together and save a seat for Syd. On our way through the lobby, we saw several police officers taking statements from classmates wherever they could find a place to sit. I waved at Ty as we hustled by.

It turned out we didn't need to rush—Syd had snagged a table for eight and was shooing away anyone who tried to take the empty seats. I sat down across from Syd while Ricky and Marco chose seats next to her.

Marco had just ordered two bottles of sparkling wine for the table when Chance stopped at the chair to my right.

"Is this seat taken?"

I smiled up at him. "It is now."

Chance looked temporarily crestfallen until I poked him. "I meant by you."

Chance sighed as he sank into the seat. "Sorry, I'm still finishing up that last brief and my brain hasn't slipped into banter mode yet." He reached for the glass of sparkling wine that the waiter poured for him. "This will help though." He closed his eyes and drained the glass, then held it out for more.

"Hey, slow down! That's not your everyday swill, Wolf!" Marco cried out as he watched Chance drain his glass a second time.

"Relax, I needed that to decompress."

Marco rolled his eyes. "As long as you're enjoying it."

Chance grabbed the bottle and poured himself a third glass before the waiter could rush over. "What is this? It's really good."

Marco peered at me. "Let's see if Kat can tell us anything about the wine."

I grinned and first held the wine up to the light. "Hmm, nice color and it has a yeasty aroma." I took a tiny sip. "Mmm, I taste citrus, spiced apple, and toasted almond." I considered for a moment. "It's a Mumm from Napa, but I'm not sure...is it one of the DVX Reserves?"

Marco grinned. "You got it. I tell you, Kat, you have a great palate. You should work with wines."

I looked down sheepishly. "I've always thought it would be fun to work at a vineyard."

Marco looked at me. "Let's talk after the weekend is over."

I gaped but couldn't ask any more questions as we were joined by Cal Jr., along with Brad and Shannon.

Cal Jr. plopped down in the empty seat to my left and eyed me with interest. "How you doing, Kat?"

He reached for the wine bottle and filled a water goblet to the rim. Marco's eyes bulged in incredulity at the selfishness. I opened my mouth to reply, but Cal Jr. continued without waiting for a response. "I saw you walking down to the pool earlier and noticed your limp. You know, if you become a member at The Mercury, I can set you up with a personal trainer who will get you limber and strong really fast."

Ricky yelped, "That's great, Cal! Marco and I finished the obstacle course and won the membership at The Mercury. Since Marco is already a member, I told Kat she had to join the gym with me."

Cal frowned. "The Mercury is not merely 'a gym,', Micky." Ricky opened his mouth to correct him but Cal Jr. barreled on. "The Mercury is the premier exercise facility in northeastern Massachusetts. We have the most high-tech equipment and best personal training staff in New England. We are not 'a gym'." Ricky swallowed nervously and nodded. "Now that you understand, I guess I'll see you at The Mercury." He turned his back to Ricky and faced me, draping his arm around the back of my chair. "So,

Kat, when would you like me to schedule your first training session? I don't usually take personal clients anymore but I'd make an exception for you."

I surreptitiously slid forward in my chair to create some personal space. "Uh, thanks Cal, but I need to check with my physical therapist and doctor first to make sure what I can do. I'd hate to mess up all the progress I've made."

Cal Jr. nodded his head vigorously. "That's a good idea." He pulled out a business card and wrote a number on it before handing it to me. "This is my personal number. Call me after you speak with the therapist and then we can put something on the books. I can even work with your therapist to come up with an individualized plan for you." He looked me up and down in a way that made me feel dirty. "I heard you got hurt on the job. Is that right?"

I didn't normally like to talk about myself and I especially didn't like to talk about getting stabbed by some hopped-up meth-head with people I barely knew. I just nodded curtly and then swiveled to face Chance. Cal Jr. leaned in even closer to me so that I could feel his hot breath on my neck.

"I'm glad you're okay now, Kat. I really think I can help you fully recover," he whispered, dousing me with his sour breath.

I shuddered a little but tried to cover it up with a cough. "You really helped MJ, too, didn't you, Cal? I saw her Friday night before… well, you know. Anyway, she looked great."

Cal sat back in his chair and eyed me appraisingly. "Who told you that?" he asked in a menacing tone.

I pretended to think for a moment. "MJ told me herself. She said she never could have gotten into such good shape without her trainer, Cal Mercury, Jr."

"Hmm, yeah, I helped her a long time ago, out in LA." He sat back up and looked around the table. "She was crazy, though. She thought me training her meant that we would be together. Romantically." He glanced sideways at me. "I set her straight, though."

I nodded agreeably. "Had you seen her recently?"

Cal Jr. looked confused. "I saw her here at the reunion on Friday night, just like everyone else."

"I didn't know if you still kept in touch, that's all. I thought you might still consult with her on her exercise program."

Cal bristled. "I haven't trained her in years which is why she was starting to look flabby again. Probably all those orgies and alcohol." He shook his head. "She changed, Kat. She wasn't like she used to be in high school."

I didn't think he had even noticed her in high school, but maybe I was wrong.

At the mention of orgies, I saw Brad cringe and Shannon elbow him in the side. I wondered what that was all about, but wanted to keep talking to Cal.

"Orgies? Oh, my, I never heard anything about that."

Cal Jr. was nodding his head up and down. "Yeah. Where do you think she got all that stuff for her books? It was from her own personal life. She actually lived all that sex stuff."

I was shocked into silence, as was the rest of the table; they had all been listening intently to our conversation. Shannon cleared her throat and asked, "Can we please change the topic? It's so depressing to talk about MJ now that she's dead." She looked around. "And really, sex and orgies are not appropriate topics when we're eating."

Cal Jr. huffed at Shannon and then looked across the room. He abruptly pushed his chair back, nearly toppling it over. "Later, everyone,"

80

he leered at me, "and Kat. I've got more people to see." He then sauntered across three tables over, grabbed an empty chair, and wedged himself in between Juan and Ned.

Everyone sighed and started talking about the rest of the weekend. Brad asked Ricky about his presentation and Ricky launched into an animated explanation about gaming and the world of business.

When he paused to take a breath, Marco piped up, "Don't forget to come to my wine tasting right after lunch, too. I brought some delicious bottles to share and would love to hear everyone's opinion." He looked across the table at me. "Especially yours, Kat."

I blushed and Chance looked at me with eyebrows raised. I managed to mumble, "Uh, sure thing, Marco," before taking a big bite of my cheeseburger. Ricky glared daggers at me across the table.

Chance smirked at Marco. "Don't worry, Marco. I'll be there, too."

Marco rolled his eyes and turned to talk to Ricky about the obstacle course. This led to the two of them recounting how Marco had to pull Ricky up the climb-over wall and how Ricky had to talk Marco through the narrow tunnel when he got stuck. They painted a vivid picture and we all chuckled at their tales.

Sometimes, hanging with old friends was really nice.

Chapter Eighteen

After dessert was served and the plates were cleared, the "Recognition" portion of the event began. Amelia, President of the Alumni Association, presented certificates of achievement to a large number of classmates. She had created certificates in such inane categories as "Traveled Farthest," "Most Kids," "Most Facebook Connections."

I really didn't want to stay for the presentation but everyone else seemed to be enjoying themselves. Unfortunately, Syd had chosen a table near the front and it was impossible for me to sneak away unnoticed, so I sat and let my thoughts wander as Amelia droned on.

Cal Jr. received a "Trained the Most Celebrities" certificate. Marco got "Finds Best New Wines", and Syd got "Best Artist". Even Chance received a certificate for "Best Hair"— that was right on the money, if you asked me. I was silently admiring his dark, wavy, award-winning hair and thinking how I'd like to run my hands through it when I heard Amelia call my name. I sat forward abruptly, jolted out of my very pleasant reverie. As Syd and Ricky urged me on, I staggered up to the stage, completely clueless what my certificate was for. I really needed to stop daydreaming so much.

Amelia beamed at me. "Kat, I thought and thought about what to give you. So, because of your past jobs, I decided that as a former investigator…" Amelia cupped her hand around the side of her mouth and said to the audience, "and with your name…"

I began to realize I was not going to like whatever this was.

"…I would like to present you with the 'Most Curious' certificate."

I took the piece of paper she handed me and gave a brief wave to the audience before rushing back to my seat.

"Why are you scowling, Kat?" Syd whispered.

"These awards are just another way for Amelia to condescend to the rest of us," I grumbled.

I must have been louder than I thought. Shannon picked up her certificate and waved it around, "If anyone should be upset, it's me. "Best Homemaker? Really? I wasn't even in your graduating class. She didn't need to give me a certificate at all." She threw the certificate down on the dirty plate in front of her. "I have other accomplishments, if Amelia Smythe-Jones-Beauregard would ever deign to ask." She started enumerating her accomplishments on her fingers. "I'm writing a book. I ran Brad's campaign for mayor. I'm meeting with party officials to map out Brad's campaign for state representative. I manage a housekeeper and nanny to keep up with all the housework and kids."

I sat back and wondered if I sounded that sullen.

Mayor Brad leaned over and rubbed her arm. "You do a lot, Shannon." He glared up at Amelia on the stage and then looked at me. He spat out, "I agree with you, Kat. Amelia is the same old, mean-spirited bitch she always was back in high school." He pushed his chair back from the table. "Maybe I'll go have a word with her to let her know just what I think of her little certificates."

We were shocked into silence as he labored to his feet.

Shannon grabbed his hand and smiled fondly up at Brad. "I'm not really upset, Brad. Amelia is meaningless to me." She glanced at me. "I was just trying to commiserate with Kat, you know, make her feel better."

Ricky, who had won "Best Tech Geek" watched as Mayor Brad sat down slowly and wagged his finger at me. "Don't you get all negative on us, Kat," he said sternly. "This was just a bit of fun and entertainment during lunch. You, too, Shannon." He looked over at Chance and fluffed his own hair. "Besides, I'm the one who should be upset. Who would *ever* say that his hair is better than mine?"

Everyone at the table erupted in laughter, as Ricky had intended. I felt my scowl melting away and reached for my champagne flute. After a few more sips, I relaxed even more. Cal Jr. had left his water goblet more than half full of wine and I contemplated pouring the remainder into my glass.

Marco was checking his phone, which had just beeped. "Damn! I need to go make sure the room is set up for the wine tasting and the wine is open and breathing." He looked around the table. "Will you all be there?"

Cal Jr. popped up behind my chair and interjected, "Not me. I gotta make sure Zeke has me all set up for the Iron Man fitness class." He patted his stomach and looked pointedly at Marco's midsection. "My body is a temple. You'll never lose that flab around your gut if you keep drinking, no matter how hard you train." Marco for once was at a loss for words. He looked sadly down at his stomach, which was not flabby at all, not that I had noticed.

Ricky shook his head and slapped and the table, jolting me out of my pleasant thoughts about Marco's body. "I have my own presentation in the Sunset Room. I better go check that they got all the laptops set up. I plan on conducting a hands-on class for my Advertising with Advanced Games presentation." He jumped out of his seat and jogged out of the room. I noticed that everyone at the luncheon was starting to disperse.

"Isn't anybody coming to my wine tasting?" Marco asked, looking at me, Shannon, and Mayor Brad hopefully.

Brad opened his mouth and I was sure he was going to say "yes" but Shannon cut him off. "We really can't, Marco. Sorry. It's just not a good idea for the Mayor to be seen drinking alcohol."

Chance chuckled. "Most politicians I've met consume a lot of adult beverages."

Shannon looked pointedly at Chance. "Brad isn't like most politicians. He'll go far with his moral principles, you'll see." Chance opened his mouth to reply but Shannon cut him off and turned to Cal Jr. "By the way, how is your father, Cal? I heard he was in shock after seeing MJ's dead body?"

Cal Jr. regarded Shannon distastefully. "He's fine, or he will be if he ever sobers up. He needs to man up!" Cal Jr. flexed his muscles and then walked purposefully out of the room. I tried to hide my laughter with a cough.

Shannon also tried to hide her smirk as she checked her phone. "Brad, we – that is , you – have a conference call with that builder who wants to develop the luxury condos on Horace Park."

Mayor Brad nodded absently, pushed up his glasses with his forefingers, and took his wife's hand as they left the room, nodding good-bye to us.

I looked questioningly at Syd. "I didn't know they were developing Horace Park into condos."

Syd shrugged. "That's all you got out of that whole conversation?" She shook her head at me. "Yeah, they've been talking about it for years and now there are enough people on the Town Council who will make money off the deal, so it's bound to go through."

I looked concerned. "That's a shame. There are a lot of houses behind Horace Park that will lose their view of the harbor."

Marco stopped looking at his stomach and cut in, "That's progress." He sighed in disgust, "and greed and corruption. Welcome to the small-town political process." He frowned. "People better show up for my wine tasting."

Syd smiled at him and rested her hand on his arm. "Don't worry, Marco. Where there's wine, there's Kat. And Chance already said he'd be there, too." I frowned at her and started to say I was going to Ricky's presentation, when she shook her head sharply at me. "I'll be the martyr who doesn't understand one word of what Ricky is talking about. Someone better pour me a big glass of wine for the road!"

Marco sighed exaggeratedly. "Okay, then. Stop by the wine tasting on your way and I'll hook you up. The rest of you better be thirsty—I brought a lot of wine and I'm not bringing any back to the warehouse!"

Chance put his arm around the back of my chair. "That sounds like a challenge, Milano."

Marco eyed Chance's arm on my chair. "Take it any way you like, Wolf." He smirked, pushed back his chair, and walked out.

I punched Chance's arm lightly. "Why do you antagonize him?"

"It's fun." Chance shrugged. "Don't worry. Marco can dish it out just as well as he takes it. We were best friends until we both went away to college in different states. I think we'll be friends again now that we're both back in Harmony." He pushed his chair back. "Well, ladies, this was fun. Kat, I will meet you in the Blue Room at 2:00. Wait – that's closed. Any idea where the tasting has been moved to? We should have asked Marco."

Syd and I shook our heads.

"I want to double-check to make sure my email with the brief went through and then I can really celebrate the end of my law career for the rest of the weekend. Can you text me the new location when you find it?" Chance held his hand out for my phone and entered his mobile number, eliciting a raised eyebrow and self-satisfied smile from Syd.

I looked at Chance and asked, "Why don't you check your email on your phone?"

Chance stood up and looked at his watch. "Save me a seat. I only have ten minutes to get to my room and check my computer." He shrugged and called over his shoulder, "My email app is a bit glitchy on my phone. I've been meaning to get that fixed."

Syd waved as he walked away. Then she leaned back in her chair and looked at me.

"What?"

"This is certainly turning into an interesting weekend for you— someone who didn't even want to come."

I shook my head. "You're too much. And what the hell was that all about? You know Ricky is expecting both of us at his presentation."

"You don't give yourself enough credit, Kat. Chance didn't ask Marco where the wine tasting had moved; he waited so he had an excuse to give you his cell phone number. And, Marco has made it clear that he would like you to work for him in some capacity – and who knows what else he wants to offer you. There is *no way* you're skipping the wine tasting now! I just wish I could be there!"

I just shook my head at her. "Let's go now so I can try to get seats for Chance and me in the front."

Syd smiled approvingly, then put a restraining hand on my arm. "Wait. I wanted to tell you that I spoke with Ty after my massage."

I looked at her inquisitively. "How is he? I'm sure he's running on fumes. I bet he didn't get any sleep last night."

"Yeah, he's exhausted but they are pushing hard to get statements from everyone and watch all the video footage to confirm alibis before the reunion ends and people start checking out. They need to collate all the info – well, you know the drill."

I nodded thoughtfully. "Has he turned up any motives or suspects?"

Syd shook her head. "No, and he's frustrated. It seems like nobody can confirm anyone else's alibi and nobody seems to have really known anything about MJ since she left town."

"That's not true. Juan saw her a quite a few times in LA, and Cal Jr. trained her, and at one point, was living with her." Syd looked suitably shocked at these revelations. I looked around and saw Sunny standing out on the patio, talking to Mindy. "She also dated Mindy's brother, Xavier, and Sunny saw her and some young guy, who I think was Xavier, when she worked as a personal baker on that luxury yacht."

Syd stared at me open-mouthed. "You have certainly gotten more info out of our classmates than Ty has. I think you need to fill him in."

I looked at my watch. "I will. After the wine tasting." I stood up hastily. "Come on! I want to get good seats, and you need to get wine to make it through Ricky's presentation."

Syd stood up and we walked quickly out of the room.

Chapter Nineteen

It turned out they had moved the wine tasting to the Paul Revere Room, a smaller meeting room down another hallway, as the Blue Room was still cordoned off by crime scene tape and a police guard. I texted Chance the new location and then looked for two seats. I wasn't early enough to get seats in the front row and ended up having to sit in the middle of the third row. I got some dirty looks as I held a seat for Chance and had to turn a few people away, but I had promised.

Marco stepped up to the podium and flashed his mischievous smile. He looked out over the packed room— there must have been 25 classmates and spouses jammed into the small meeting room— and locked eyes with me. I felt a shiver go through my body.

I heard more grumbling about the empty seat next to me. It seemed as though Chance might have bailed on the tasting and I was about to give the seat up when he finally showed up and had to squeeze down the row. His disarming smile was enough to quiet the grumblers. Marco shook his head slightly, turned back to face the center of the room, and launched into his presentation.

There was a bit of commotion in the back and I turned around to see what was causing the ruckus. Of course, it was Mindy and Julian. They had also come in late and were dragging chairs in since there were no more empty seats. Mindy did not look happy about having to carry her own chair or sitting in the back but her husband was obliviously reading something on his phone. Mindy caught me peering at her and sneered in her oh-so-friendly manner. I looked around some more, hoping to see Sunny, but she was not in the crowd. I wanted to ask her some follow-up questions after our earlier talk.

Considering that he was often a little bit goofy, Marco's manner during the wine tasting surprised me. He was the consummate professional and conducted the wine tasting like an informal seminar. He wasn't kidding either—he had brought *a lot* of wine. To be fair, he brought spittoons as well but I was not about to spit out such high-quality wine. I don't think anyone else used the spittoons either.

Marco beamed at the attendees. "I'm going to conduct this seminar just like any other wine tasting you may have attended. I brought four of the most popular types of wines in each major category— a white, a sparkling, a rosé, and a red. The criteria I used to choose these particular wines is that they had to be rated at 90 or above by *Wine Spectator* and they had to cost under $30 per bottle." A low murmur ran through the room. "I wanted to make sure you could taste good, affordable wines and compare them to wines of the same variety you may already drink at home." He smiled at the room. "I may just change the way you drink wine."

He grabbed the microphone off the holder and stepped to a table laden with wine. "As many of you know, my family has a small vineyard and we have been in wine sales and distribution for over 50 years. I have been learning about wine since my mama handed me my first sippy cup." He paused while everyone chuckled. "When I took over the business, I wanted to expand internationally and bring in some remarkable, affordable, yet highly rated wines to add to our offerings." He pointed to the wines. "For today, I will be pouring wines from the Napa Valley in California to show you how easy it is to get good wine." He picked up a bottle. "First, we'll start with a Beringer Chardonnay Napa Valley Reserve, vintage 1995. It scored a 97 and costs about $29." Murmurs and nods spread through the room.

He picked up another bottle with a longer neck and he heard a slight titter and some "Oohs." "Yes, we will be trying a sparkling wine today as well. This is the Domaine Chandon Brut Napa County Cuvée 494 Reserve. It has a rating of 92 and costs around $24." He placed the bottle on the table and turned back to the group. "To be honest, I prefer the Mumm sparklings from Napa but they do cost slightly more than this Domaine Chandon. I suggest you do a mini taste test at home and decide which one you prefer for the price."

"Next, we'll move on to an off-dry rosé, the Cornerstone Corallina Rosé Stepping Stone Napa Valley. It scored a 90 with a very reasonable price of $20. I think those of you who have turned your nose up at rosé wines will be pleasantly surprised. This is mainly because we are returning to the French style of rosé wines that are dry or off-dry and away from those overly sweet and highly sugared varieties that taste more like white zinfandels."

He took a step along the table and picked up another bottle. "This will be our final wine of the day—or at this tasting, at least." He grinned and held the bottle up as the audience chuckled. "We will taste Chateau Montelena Estate Cabernet Sauvignon Napa Valley. It was rated a 97 and costs about $30."

Marco pointed to a man I thought was part of the hotel waitstaff. "This is Giovanni. He is the Milano Winery vintner. He has made all our wines for the past ten years and offered to help out today." Giovanni waved at the group and we obliged with some appreciative applause. Marco stage-whispered, "I didn't want anyone to wait too long for a pour of wine." Giovanni and Marco moved through the room, pouring the chardonnay. When everyone had about half a glass—a far more generous pour than traditional wine tastings—Marco began demonstrating the correct way to taste wine.

"First, look at the wine from above and the side to see the complete color and to make sure it is clear." Marco paused while everyone raised their glasses to appreciate the clear, pale gold liquid.

"Next, swirl the wine around in the glass to see if it has 'legs,'" Marco demonstrated the technique with his own glass. "In other words, leaves a trail on the side of the glass. Good legs means the wine has more alcohol and is usually bigger, riper, and more mouth-filling."

"Now, hover your nose over the glass and take a few quick sniffs and try to determine which fruits, flowers, herbs, and other scents you detect." He paused again as the audience sniffed the wine and hesitantly suggested what scents they caught, some of which were so off-base I had to smother a laugh.

"Finally, sip the wine as if sucking through a straw to aerate it. Try to identify the fruit, flower, herb, mineral, and barrel flavors to determine if the wine is balanced, complex, or harmonious." Most of my classmates looked puzzled by this, so Marco and Giovanni demonstrated the technique and got them started by describing a few of the notes they would likely taste as they sipped.

After each tasting, Marco stood by the whiteboard and asked us to share our tasting notes, which he scribbled under the name of each bottle. People were hesitant at first, but I jumped right in and gave my opinion. Others relaxed when they realized they weren't being judged – and with each successive bottle of wine – and by the end, we were all shouting out flavors like pear, honeysuckle, or currants. This brought on lively discussions between the participants and the hour flew by. Marco was very skilled in teasing out the nuances that the participants had tasted in the wines.

Marco and Giovanni kept opening and pouring bottles. They also moved through the room to more deeply discuss each wine with the attendees. I wholeheartedly shared my thoughts on each wine we tasted, but Chance mostly just agreed or disagreed without venturing his own opinions. I noticed that he carefully took notes, though, and I wondered whether I would see some of these wines on the Two Cups wine menu.

At the end of the tasting, Marco stood next to the white board that was filled with our tasting notes. Everyone took out their phones to take pictures of the board so they would remember later. We had consumed a lot of wine.

Beringer Chardonnay Napa Valley Reserve	Domaine Chandon Brut Napa County Cuvée 494 Reserve	Cornerstone Corallina Rosé Stepping Stone Napa Valley	Chateau Montelena Estate Cabernet Sauvignon Napa Valley
Pear	Pear	Great pink color	Ripe red fruit flavors
Melon	Vanilla	Well-balanced	Smooth finish
Nuts	Hazelnut	Crisp acidity	Better with more aging
A slight meaty edge	Yeast	Delicately rich fruit	
	Smooth and creamy	Raspberry	
		Spice	
		Smoky vanilla	
🍷🍷🍷🍷🍷	🍷🍷🍷🍷🍷	🍷🍷🍷🍷🍷	🍷🍷🍷🍷🍷

At the end, the participants voted and agreed that all four bottles should receive five out of five wine glasses, which Marco called the Milano Wine Rating Method. 🍷🍷🍷🍷🍷.

When everyone had their notes carefully tucked away, Marco invited the attendees to help themselves to the rest of the wine. I had another two glasses of the sparkling before I finally put my wine glass down. I felt a little woozy. Marco had been very heavy-handed while pouring the wine, especially in my glass.

I had a few minutes before I had to meet Syd on the patio for high tea. Marco had let us all keep our wine glasses with the Milano Vineyards logo imprinted on them. He pushed two more glasses into my hands. "Take these for Syd and Ricky. Everyone could always use more wine glasses."

I gathered up the three wine glasses and turned to Chance. "I don't want to risk breaking the glasses at high tea. I'm going to run them up to my room first. Will you tell Syd and Ricky that I'll be right down?"

Chance shook his head and tried to stifle a yawn. "I wasn't planning on going to high tea. Especially now after all this wine." He looked pointedly at Marco who grinned and walked away to answer some wine questions from a group of participants. "I'm going to grab a quick nap and then maybe do some more wine research for the wine bar." He looked at Marco and shook his head. "You would never guess he knows so much about wine."

I grinned and nodded in agreement. "Okay, we can head upstairs together then."

Chance cocked an eyebrow at me and chuckled as I blushed crimson.

Chapter Twenty

Chance and I rode the elevator up together in companionable silence. When we got to his floor, he stepped out of the elevator but leaned back in before it could close.

"Meet you at happy hour?" he asked with a lopsided grin.

I nodded and smiled. "If I can sober up by then." I looked down and realized that, in an alcohol haze, I had only grabbed my glasses and forgotten the two I had set aside for Syd and Ricky. "Damn!" I cursed softly.

Chance looked at me curiously. "What's the matter?"

"I just realized I forgot Syd and Ricky's glasses. They'll be pissed if they're not waiting for them in the room when they get back. I'm going to run back to the Paul Revere Room and grab them, but I'll still meet you at happy hour," I grinned lopsidedly, "I hope."

Chance grinned back at me. "Do you want me to go with you?"

I shook my head. "No, thanks. I'm just going to zip down and back."

Chance chuckled, "Unless Marco talks your ear off."

I smiled at him and Chance let the door close and I rode up alone to the penthouse floor. I immediately hit the lobby button and rode the elevator back down, thinking salacious thoughts about Chance. When I got there, I tried not to make eye contact with anyone so I wouldn't have to chat. I discovered that I also needed to use the ladies' room, but I didn't want to use the facilities down here. Too many bad memories.

I slipped into the Paul Revere Room and tried to slink over to where I had been sitting. I was lucky and only Giovanni was in there cleaning up. He waved at me and continued boxing up spare wine glasses and packing up the remaining unopened bottles of wine. I waved back at him and pointed at the wine glasses I had left behind. He smiled and waved again. I wondered where Marco had gone. He didn't seem like the type of person to leave his staff to clean up while he went to have fun but I didn't really know him all that well.

I grabbed the glasses and headed back to the elevator. Fortunately, I was able to make my way without any classmate encounters and I rode the elevator up to the penthouse floor alone. Thoughts of Chance and Marco kept flitting through my imagination and I was still smiling while I walked down the corridor toward my room. As I approached the turn in the hall, I saw that the fire door was propped open and thought how dangerous that was. I shook my head and chastised myself for being such a worrywart and always thinking of the worst that could happen. Then as I walked closer, I realized I hadn't even thought of the worst case situation— there was a limp, bloody hand caught between the door and the door frame.

I raced over, pulling my phone from my pocket. I cautiously pushed on the door, just far enough to see a female body, her head and mass of blonde curls spilling over the first step. I quickly scanned the hallway behind me to make sure I was alone as I did not want to be the next victim. I was sure this attack must be related to MJ's murder because the woman had a steak knife – which looked identical to the one used to kill MJ— sticking out of her back.

When I was certain the killer wasn't creeping up behind me, I dialed 9-1-1 and crouched down to check for a pulse. I nearly jumped for joy when I felt a faint beat. I took a moment to recover my breath and to report the situation to the 9-1-1 operator. The operator told me that an ambulance and the police were en route to my location. I knew that most of the Harmony Police Department were still in the hotel, so I hoped they would respond quickly.

Keeping my phone pressed to my ear, I moved the limp hand and wadded up my notes and pamphlets from the wine tasting to use them to wedge the door open. I carefully went down a couple of steps, watching to avoid blood or any other trace evidence. I sat down on the top stair next to the body and gently lifted the blonde curls away from the face. Damn it!

Chapter Twenty-One

"Sunny," I cried. Sunny's eyes fluttered a little and she struggled to talk, but I couldn't make out a word she was saying. I heard the elevator doors open and footsteps rushing down the hallway toward me as well as pounding footsteps coming up the stairs. I smoothed Sunny's hair back and made soothing sounds as I heard Ty's voice.

"Kat?" he thundered. "Kat, where are you?"

Suddenly, Ty was standing in the doorway of the emergency stairs, surrounded by police officers, and others were below me in the stairwell. The ambulance workers were moments behind the police and roughly pushed them, and me, out of the way to begin work on Sunny. I let Ty guide me out of the stairwell.

"What happened?" he demanded.

I shook my head. "I don't know. I was heading back to the room to drop off wine glasses," I looked down at my hands and realized they were empty. I frantically cast my eyes about and saw the glasses lying on the carpet, a few feet away. I pointed at them and Ty motioned to one of his men to pick them up. I barely registered that he dropped the glasses into evidence bags.

"Continue," he motioned with his hands.

"There's not much else. I saw the fire door was propped open and thought how dangerous that could be. I was heading over to close it and I saw a bloody hand. I slowly opened the door and saw the body— Sunny's body! I quickly checked the area before I called 9-1-1 and I checked for vital signs." I looked up at Ty hopefully. "There was a pulse and she blinked her eyes a little when I said her name. Do you think she'll be okay?"

Ty led me further down the hall to my suite as the ambulance workers loaded Sunny onto a gurney and rolled it toward the elevator at a fast clip. One of them caught Ty's eyes and waggled his hand, fingers spread. He sighed, "Let's go in here so you can sit down."

"I'm fine, Ty. That EMT did not look very hopeful."

Ty looked at me with concern. "I'm not going to sugarcoat this, Kat. You were a soldier and a cop. She was stabbed in the back and the knife went all the way in. It could go either way but I think we have to prepare for the worst." He scrubbed his face with his hands.

I sank to the couch in the suite. "Damn it!" I exhaled noisily. "I just spoke with Sunny this morning and I was thinking it might not be such a bad thing to stay in Harmony. People seem nicer now than when I was younger."

Ty looked at me accusingly. "You weren't investigating this case, were you?"

I quickly shook my head. "Of course not. I'm not a cop anymore. I was just speaking with people at the reunion." I looked at him innocently. "How is the investigation going?"

Ty looked at me suspiciously. "Fine."

I looked around the room, sighed, and then blurted out, "In the course of talking to people, I did find out some information about MJ if you're interested."

Ty let out an exasperated breath. "Kat!"

"I know, I know," I said apologetically. "People just like to tell me things."

Ty pulled out his notebook and pointed at me. "Normally, I wouldn't take hearsay from just anyone, but I know you were a good cop and wouldn't share anything if it wasn't important."

"Absolutely, Ty. I just want MJ's murderer," I looked toward the suite door, "and Sunny's attacker to be caught, no matter who it is."

Ty sighed and waved his hand at me to continue. I recounted all that I had learned in the last eighteen hours about MJ, Xavier, Mindy, Cal Jr., and Sunny's cryptic comments. I also told him everything Juan had shared about MJ and her lifestyle.

Ty sighed again as I finished my narrative and leaned his head back on the sofa. He jumped to his feet as the door flew open and Syd walked in angrily, already berating me before she even made it through the foyer.

Chapter Twenty-Two

"Were you ever planning to show up for tea, Kat? Ricky was coming late because he had to break down the room, and Marco didn't show at all, so I've been sitting on the patio by myself for half an hour watching the cucumber sandwiches go limp. You know I don't like sitting alone and I especially don't like tea – " She stopped short when she spotted Ty and the blood on my hands and clothes. "OMG!" she shrieked. "Are you alright?" She tried to rush to my side but Ty jumped up from the couch and stepped between us, blocking Syd from touching me, as two policemen followed her into the suite.

I said, "Not my blood" just as Ty whispered "Evidence," to Syd before turning his wrath on the police officers. "What part about 'guard the door' didn't you two understand?"

They looked at each other and back at Ty, trying to form words. Finally, the older deputy stammered, "She's your wife, sir, and this is her room." He looked again at the other deputy. "We didn't think you meant *her*."

Ty walked up to within two inches of the older deputy's face. "'Don't let anyone in' means 'don't let *anyone* in'." He looked at his wife and his face softened a little. "I don't think my wife is the killer either, but she could have been." He then looked over at me. "And my witness could have been sharing sensitive information, did you ever think of that?"

The two police officers nodded at Ty and the younger one visibly gulped. "Yes, sir." They turned to Syd, and the young one said "Ma'am, could you please follow us out?"

Syd looked at Ty incredulously, then glared at the younger officer. "Don't you 'ma'am' me! I will *not* follow you out. I have some vital information to share with the Chief of Police.

Ty looked up at the ceiling and appeared to be counting to ten. "Officers, I can see that this will not go smoothly. She can stay." He looked at them. "Send Officer Freely in for Ms. Snow's clothes."

Syd bent around Ty and gaped at me. "Why are you covered in blood?"

I quickly filled her in on finding Sunny.

Syd sunk onto the opposite couch and stared open-mouthed at Ty and me. Finally, she turned to Ty accusingly. "You were on the football team in high school."

He looked at Syd, then me, bewildered. "What does that have to do with any of this?"

She scrunched up her face and scowled at him. "Were you one of the guys who 'had sex' or whatever, with a drunk girl in the locker room?"

Ty's eyes opened wide and he stared at Syd, at a loss for words.

I tried to calm Syd down. "Come on, Syd. Why would you think Ty would have had anything to do with that?"

Syd was breathing hard. "I just had an interesting conversation with Bo before Ricky's presentation. I ran into him after I saw you, Ty, in the lobby." She shook her head. "I mean, I literally bumped right into him. I would have fallen over if he hadn't caught me."

Ty sighed. "What does you bumping into Bo or a drunk girl having sex have to do with this case?"

"I'm getting to it," Syd snapped, then put her hand on his arm in apology. "I asked where Amelia was and he said they were splitting up to attend as many events as possible. He told me Amelia went to Iron Man Fitness. By then, we were near the Blue Room." Syd blinked away a tear. "We saw the floor stand with a sign for MJ's *Author Talk* pushed back against the wall." Syd took a deep breath.

"When I looked up at Bo, I saw his cheeks were moist from tears. I was confused because I didn't think they knew each other in high school. They certainly did not run in the same circles." Syd looked over at Kat. "I thought, 'What would Kat do?', and then I realized you would talk to him about why he was so upset." Ty leaned over and squeezed her shoulder. She smiled tightly at him. "I asked him how well he knew MJ. He told me she was his math tutor in high school and then again later at Boston University. It seems they both went there."

Syd got up and began pacing. "Bo told me that MJ only agreed to tutor him in high school because she had a huge crush on one of the other football players and he told her he would hook her up. He lied and told her he tried," Syd shook her head, "but he didn't even try because he didn't want her to be distracted from tutoring him."

Syd stopped by the window and looked out. "Bo said that MJ had changed a lot in high school. She was still shy but she didn't have a lot of friends and was always watching people and analyzing them. He said she went to trauma groups and later would write down what people had said about their past experiences."

Kat spoke up, "That's really weird."

Syd nodded her head. "I thought that was weird, too. He said that she told him she was observing human behavior so that her writing would be more authentic. Bo said that MJ had written about the two of them in one of her books." Syd turned around to face them. "Apparently, they hooked up when Amelia spent a semester in Spain. They had agreed to 'take a break' while she was gone but MJ had been pretty serious about Bo and didn't take it well when Amelia came back and he dumped her."

Ty was furiously writing down everything Syd said in his notebook. Kat shook her head and mused aloud, "I wonder which book?"

Syd chuckled. "I wondered the same thing but he wouldn't tell me."

Ty looked up. "I still don't see where this is going. What does this have to do with MJ's murder?"

Syd came back and sat next to Ty. "I'm getting to the important part now, hon." She shook her head in exasperation at Kat. "After he declined to tell me which encounter related to him, he said that she had also written about something in *Curious on the Gridiron* that happened to another girl at our high school. In a locker room. He didn't know how MJ had found out about it though."

Kat looked stunned. "That really happened?"

Syd nodded. "Yup. I totally lost my temper with him then and asked how he could have done something like that to a girl back in high school. I really let him have it."

Ty had stopped writing and was staring at Syd. Then he cleared his throat and indicated she should continue.

"Bo insisted that he didn't do anything, that he wasn't even there. He looked really ashamed though when he admitted that he did watch the video. He said it was clear that the girl had been drugged and it was not consensual."

Syd shuddered. "I pressed him about who the girl was and who the rapists were. He wouldn't tell me. He said that the girl seemed to be doing well and the guys now had lives and families that he didn't want destroyed if the truth about the past came to light."

Kat leaned in. "It did come to light though. In the book and the movie."

"I know. I told Bo that those boys had committed rape and that they should pay for what they had done to that girl. Bo said he thought that

104

MJ was trying to make them pay by publishing the 'secret' for the world to read."

The room was quiet except for the sound of Ty's pen scratching across his notebook page. When he finished, he put the pen in his pocket and the notebook on his lap. The silence stretched on a few moments until the door opened quietly and Officer Freely came in with some evidence bags. Ty looked at Kat and smiled grimly. "You know the drill."

Kat got up and started walking toward one of the bedrooms with the Officer. Suddenly, Syd jumped up and angrily shouted, "It was rape. They are all criminals. Those who did it and those who watched the recording and did nothing about it." Kat stopped to listen to Syd.

Ty put his hands on his wife's shoulders. "This was good information, Syd, and may even be related to the case, but why would you ever think I would have had anything to do with any of that?"

A few tears slid down Syd's cheek. "Bo wouldn't tell me who had participated. Just that it happened in our junior year of high school and that the whole football team had seen the recording at one of their parties."

Ty looked at her and then pulled her into his arms. "If you remember, I spent all of my free time my senior year with a certain artist during high school. I never hung out with the guys on the team except to play football." He let out a sigh. "I did hear a few rumors, but I thought it was just empty talk. Maybe I am guilty of not looking into it further. Everyone knew I wouldn't accept that kind of behavior though, so they probably made a point not to share it with me."

Syd looked up at him and stepped away. She looked over toward Kat. "Who do you think the girl was? I feel badly that we don't know and couldn't have helped her at the time."

I took a deep breath. "I think it was Sunny. We know it wasn't Marla Jean based on what Bo told you. Remember how Sunny told me that she had confessed something to MJ on the yacht and that MJ then wrote about it? I think that must have been what she confessed." I looked out the window for a moment, with Officer Freely waiting patiently nearby. I slapped my forehead. "I don't know why I never put this together before, but I remember now that after those rumors came out, Sunny was out for the last two months of junior year. I heard she had mono, but she was probably too upset or scared to come to school. I remember being surprised she wasn't held back."

Syd nodded in agreement. "I remember that." She turned to Ty. "Who else was on the football team besides for you and Bo during my junior year?"

Ty scratched his chin and looked out the window while he thought about it. "There were twenty of us but if I limit it to junior and seniors, then," he counted off on his fingers, "Me, Bo, Brad, Cal Jr., Ned, Chance, Marco, Juan, Bruce, Chip, Tiny, Bobby, and Stu. The rest were mostly sophomores and a few freshmen, but we didn't hang out with them." He looked over at Kat. "The only guys here for the reunion are me, Bo, Brad, Cal Jr., Ned, Chance, Marco, and Juan."

Syd and I stared at each other until Officer Freely politely cleared her throat. I had totally forgotten I had to give up another outfit to the police. At this rate, packing to go home was going to be very easy. Luckily, if I needed anything from the hotel shops it was on Amelia and Bo. I smiled apologetically and followed Officer Freely into the bedroom.

I stripped off my clothes and put them into the paper bags. I slipped into one of the hotel's robes and pulled my hair back into a ponytail. Officer Freely nodded, picked up the evidence bag with my clothes and shoes, and walked out the door. I trailed out after her and Syd scrunched up her face as she looked at me.

"You're still bloody. You're going to take a shower, right?"

106

I rolled my eyes. "Of course, but I know Ty has to get back to his investigation and I wanted to see if he had any suggestions for who we should speak with at tonight's events." We both turned and looked at him expectantly.

Ty stared back, incredulous. He started speaking a few times and trailed off. Finally, he managed, "My suggestion is that you two, and Ricky, go home." He looked pointedly at me. "This is not your investigation and you are not police officers."

Syd and I hung our heads for a moment, then Syd lifted her chin and stared her husband straight in the eye. "We're not going home, Ty, and you can't make us. We'll be sure we stick together from now on, but we're staying, and we may just find out some more information that can help you solve the case. Most of your information has come from us anyways."

Ty sputtered then snapped his mouth closed, got up, and started heading toward the door. "I better not find you over any more bodies, Kat, or I just might arrest you."

I held my hands up in surrender. "Believe me, I don't want to find any more bodies."

Ty slammed the door as he left. I turned to go back into the bedroom and stopped in the doorway. "I'm really proud of you for standing up to Ty like that."

Syd sank onto the sofa. "I'm still shaking."

I spun and stared at her, shocked – and she raised her hands in a placating gesture. "Don't get me wrong. I'm not scared of Ty and he has never done anything that would remotely hurt me. We just almost never raise our voices at each other. We tend to compromise." She looked at me a little sheepishly. "It's why our marriage has lasted so long." She looked out the window. "He wasn't entirely wrong either. There are people getting attacked and killed here this weekend. It's not safe."

I thought for a moment. "Well, it was still a compromise. Just a loud one."

Syd chuckled and I turned once again to go scrub the day – and the blood – away. "What's next on the agenda?" I called over my shoulder.

Syd looked at her watch. "Well, high tea is over so the next event is happy hour at 6. We have a little time."

I had barely gone a step when the door flung open and Ricky stalked in dramatically. "Where the hell is Kat and why weren't either of you at tea? Marco didn't make it either and I was hoping he'd magically turn the tea into wine." He glanced back at the door to the suite. "And why are there so many cute cops in the hallway?" He looked at me quizzically. "And why are you wearing a robe? Hey, wait—is that *blood* in your hair?"

I sighed and glanced at Syd, who pointed me toward the bedroom with its en suite walk-in shower. "I'll fill him in on everything and then we'll go hit happy hour. Ricky, maybe you and I can start now."

Ricky looked from Syd to me and back with a puzzled expression. "I couldn't have missed that much in an hour."

Syd shook her head. "You have no idea."

Chapter Twenty-Three

After my shower, I dried my long hair and pulled it into a loose ponytail. I went all out and even put on some makeup, but I had to borrow most of that from Ricky's makeup case. I didn't even recognize some of what he had in there! After applying eyeliner, mascara, some blush and lipstick, I could almost see the Sharon Stone comparison. Almost. I slipped into a sundress and grabbed a light cardigan. The nights were still getting cold and I didn't want to come back up later if I needed a sweater. I wish we had made time to shop in one of the boutiques earlier, as I would like to try for glamorous just once in my life.

I walked into the suite's living room and saw that Syd was ready and starting to look impatient. I looked at my watch. "Relax, it's only 5:45. We'll make it in time for the full happy hour." Syd pulled her long, dark hair into a messy French twist and applied just a little bit of makeup.

Syd groaned. "Maybe. Ricky is taking his sweet time, too. He can't decide whether he should wear the black skinny jeans or the red skinny jeans and whether he should dress monochromatically like last night or mix it up a little." She said the last bit with exaggerated arm movements that I could totally picture Ricky making and I chuckled.

I walked to the second bedroom and rapped on the door. "Ricky, wear the black skinny jeans and a black shirt. You'll look fantastic. Like always."

He opened the door and looked at Syd in frustration. "See, that's all I wanted. I would have been ready a half-hour ago if you had been able to tell me what Kat just said." He ducked back inside and slammed the door. "Five minutes," he sang out.

Ten minutes later, Ricky strutted into the room. He was wearing black Gucci embroidered jeans, a Ralph Lauren black form-fitting shirt, a lightly patterned Ferragamo tie, and his trademark Hermés shoes. As always, he looked fantastic. Syd and I looked at our sundresses we had both bought on sale at Kohl's with our 30 percent off coupons. Mine was blue and white striped. I picked it to match my eyes and thought it went well with my pale gold hair and lightly tanned skin. Syd's dress was mint green with small white fleur-de-lis in the background that really brought out her green eyes. But still…I could tell we both felt frumpy compared to Ricky.

"Let's go, ladies. Happy hour won't wait for us to arrive!"

Syd and I rolled our eyes at each other at Ricky's implication that we were causing the delay. We strolled out of the room and down the hall, past the forensics team that was still collecting evidence. Ty deliberately turned his back as we walked by and Syd scowled at him.

Syd and I rode the elevator down in silence while Ricky chattered about his presentation and how a few classmates had approached him to ask how they could use games to promote their businesses. He had an appointment set up with Cal Jr. to talk about The Mercury on Monday, and even Mindy had asked if she could use games to promote her catering business. Finally, he could take no more of the silence and pulled us to the side as we crossed the lobby.

"Hey! There's nothing we can do for MJ, and Sunny is probably in surgery or something right now. So, buck up and remember this weekend is on Amelia and Bo."

Syd and I both tried to smile, and I felt my shoulders relax. I linked arms with Ricky and Syd as we headed toward the lounge.

When we walked in, I realized almost everyone else had decided to dress up for the evening. At least Syd and I were both wearing dresses, but a lot of men were wearing suits and quite a few of the women were dripping with jewelry and high fashion.

110

Syd and I shrugged at each other and we made our way to the bar. We spotted Chance and Marco at one corner of the bar and Marco asked if he could get us a drink. I found myself next to Chance and he smiled down at me warmly.

"You look nice. Did you have a good afternoon?" he asked.

I looked at him aghast, then realized that he, like most if not all of our classmates, hadn't yet heard about Sunny. When we parted ways on the elevator, Chance had said he was planning to rest in his room. It occurred to me I didn't know what Marco did after the wine tasting either, but I knew he left almost immediately and I remembered Ricky saying he hadn't shown up for high tea.

Chance started to look concerned, probably because I still hadn't answered him. Marco handed me a glass of white wine, which was a welcome distraction from my thoughts. While I tried to figure out how to reply, I took a huge gulp of the pale liquid and my eyes widened as the flavor hit my tongue.

"My goodness, Marco. That's delicious!"

He smirked. "I'm glad you like it. Can you tell me where it came from…" he looked at me sternly, "after you taste it properly, of course?"

I grinned and held the wine up to the light to appreciate its color. I then brought the glass to my nose and inhaled deeply before taking a tiny sip and letting it play across my tongue. When I finally swallowed, everyone in our small group was staring at me expectantly.

"It's a chardonnay from the Russian River Valley. I taste pear and apple pastry with a finish of," I pursed my mouth, "is that allspice?"

Marco beamed. "Remarkable. It's Paul Hobbs Chardonnay. Rated 93 points by *Wine Spectator*. You practically recited their description of this wine."

Chance cleared his throat. "Kat, you never answered my question. How was your afternoon?"

I pictured poor Sunny lying in a pool of blood and my pleasure in the wine evaporated. The suspicious thoughts about where Chance or Marco had been just before I discovered her – and the fact they were both on the football team junior year came flooding back. I really didn't think either of them was a rapist then or the killer now…but I couldn't be absolutely certain. As briefly as possible, I told them about finding Sunny and how she was now at the hospital, fighting for her life. Chance and Marco both looked shocked but that was easy to fake, I thought. I decided not to mention my theory that both these attacks were connected to that long-ago attack in high school.

Ricky decided to break the serious mood and blurted out, "What type of adult game do you think I should propose to Mindy for her event business? A bowling game or maybe some kind of role-playing game?"

We all stopped and stared at Ricky for a moment, then everyone burst into laughter picturing Mindy playing either type of game. This led to us speculating about what type of avatar Mindy would choose – a warrior elf or perhaps a nefarious troll.

Other classmates came to the bar and chatted with us before moving on. I spied Amelia and Bo across the room and Amelia waved at me. I noticed Bo watching Syd with trepidation – perhaps feeling that he had said too much earlier. Julian, on his ever-present mobile phone, joined them. Mindy followed Amelia's gaze to where I was standing and sneered at me. I rolled my eyes and turned my back on them.

A moment later, Brad and Shannon joined us. Marco asked if he could get them a glass of wine. Shannon looked disapprovingly at Marco. "I already told you that Brad, as Mayor, can't be seen drinking," she said, then stage-whispered, "or drunk" before returning to her normal voice, "in

112

public." She looked at all of us with a glass of wine in our hands. "You're adults now. Don't you do anything other than drink?"

Marco grinned mischievously. "Well, I import wines for a living, so, no, not really." The rest of us ignored her comment.

Shannon grimaced and shook her head. She glanced at Mayor Brad, then leaned in toward Syd and me conspiratorially, "The police told Brad, because he's the mayor, about another incident here at the hotel today."

I looked at Shannon wide-eyed. "Really? What happened?" I felt Chance shift in his seat and nudged him sharply with my elbow.

Shannon continued. "Somebody attacked Sunny, you know, the owner of the bakery? We heard she's in surgery right now, fighting for her life."

Syd murmured, "That's horrible."

Shannon nodded her head, "Yes, it is, especially the day after MJ got murdered." She looked primly at her folded hands. "Although MJ's books were so trashy, not that we read them, of course" she hastened to add. "It wouldn't surprise me in the least if some crazed fan of MJ's tried to engage her in one of those horrible sex acts she wrote about and things got out of hand."

Mayor Brad reached over and took Shannon's hand. I noticed he had a bandage on his right hand. "Calm down now, honey. You don't want your blood pressure to rise."

Shannon smiled at Mayor Brad. "I'm fine, sweetie."

I growled. "And how do you explain what happened to Sunny? She didn't have any crazed fans."

Shannon frowned. "Well, I obviously don't know, but from what I've heard, she was always a bit of a tramp back in high school." She looked around the room. "Maybe one of her ex-boyfriends wanted another go and she refused."

"That's a stretch and doesn't fit any of the evidence." I blurted out, then bit my tongue. I didn't want to let on how much I actually knew or suspected about the murder and attempted murder.

Shannon looked at me shrewdly. "Do you have some inside information that you'd like to share with the rest of us, Kat?" She paused for a moment when I didn't reply. "Oh, that's right. You were a cop until someone attacked you." My face contorted into a grimace. "Perhaps you were sticking your nose in where it didn't belong then, too."

I was so shocked that I couldn't even form words. The rest of the group was gaping at Shannon. who just smiled sweetly without acknowledging the tension she had just caused.

Chance put his hand on my arm and half rose out of his seat, but Syd recovered first. "How dare you…!"

Shannon cut her off. "Does Kat have you sticking *your* nose in where it doesn't belong, too? Or did your husband ask you to pry into everyone's lives?"

"What?" Syd sputtered.

The photographer Amelia had hired to take candid shots at the reunion chose that moment to take a picture of us. Shannon pulled Ned's arm around her and beamed at the camera – while my mouth was hanging open and Syd looked almost feral. We both plastered on a pleasant smile as he took a few more shots of our group and moved on.

Shannon whirled back toward Syd. "I saw you grilling Bo earlier on the way to Ricky's useless presentation. Mind your own business, Syd," she growled.

Chance stood up and started to move toward Shannon, while Marco raised his hands in a placating manner. "Okay, everybody, let's take a breath," he said calmly. "It is *happy* hour, after all."

Mayor Brad put his arm back around Shannon and said brightly, "Look, honey, it's the Pendletons. Let's go ask about their twins."

He tugged her gently but firmly and led her away with a shrug and a wave back at us. I gulped down the rest of my wine to Marco's obvious chagrin. Syd's glass was already empty and she furiously waved it at the bartender for a refill.

Marco raised one eyebrow at me and remarked, "That's more than $100 a bottle, you know."

I leaned back against the bar and held the cool glass up to my forehead. I looked apologetically at Marco. "Sorry. I just can't believe she said that to me." He nodded sympathetically and gestured to the bartender to refill my glass.

Syd finally got her drink and took a big swallow. "Me either. Who knew the Mayor's wife could be such a bitch?"

I pondered for a moment. "Actually, I think she was always a bit of a bitch. She was just so much younger than us that we didn't notice her. When I used to babysit for her family, she never wanted to share her toys and she didn't have a lot of friends." I looked across the room at Mayor Brad and Shannon standing in a small group, laughing and having a good time. "I guess that's what happens when those types of kids grow up."

Marco held up his glass. "Here's to not having those types of kids!"

We all toasted with him, drank our wine, and refilled our glasses.

Chapter Twenty-Four

The happy hour wound down and everyone started migrating toward the ballroom for dinner and dancing. Chance, Marco, and Ricky went ahead to get a table so we could all sit together while Syd and I headed to the ladies' room.

As I was washing my hands, one of the stalls opened and Mindy walked out. She made sure she was a few sinks away from me but then caught my eye in the mirror.

"I know what you've been doing, Kat," she snarled. "Always so nosy and you have to know everything." She reached for a paper towel to dry her hands. "Shannon told us all how you've been snooping around, gathering evidence to accuse one of us as Marla Jean's killer. I'm warning you that you had better stop immediately."

I turned defiantly toward Mindy. "Or what?" I demanded.

Mindy was momentarily taken aback. "Or you'll be sorry," she exploded. "If anyone finds out about my brother because of you, I'll make sure you…"

One of the toilets flushed and then a stall door flew open as Syd came striding out and took a stance beside me. "You'll make sure *what*, Mindy?"

Mindy looked at both of us. She closed her mouth tightly and walked quickly toward the door.

Syd called out to her retreating back, "Just as I thought, Mindy. You're a bully. Now get out or I will report your threats to my husband, the Chief of Police."

Mindy cast a furtive glance over her shoulder as she skulked out the door.

Syd and I looked at each other and burst out laughing. I snorted and leaned against a sink while Syd washed her hands.

"That look on her face was priceless. When that stall door flew open and she realized we weren't alone...I wish I had a camera."

Syd grinned. "I know. Mindy Sherwood was speechless. Probably the first time that ever happened."

"I bet her husband would have liked to see, er, hear that!"

We both started laughing again as we walked out of the ladies' room and down the hall to the ballroom.

Chapter Twenty-Five

Dinner was uneventful but enjoyable. Syd had texted Ty to see if there was any news about Sunny, but he said he hadn't received an update from the hospital yet. We were at a table for eight: me, Syd, Ricky, Marco, Chance, Amelia, Bo – everyone was back to calling him Bo, much to Amelia's chagrin – and, since Ty was too busy to join us, Cal Jr. had unfortunately claimed his seat. Cal Jr. bored us with stories about training celebrities and spoke harshly about how ungraceful they could be. Marco fascinated us—well, me, at least—with tales of bizarre rituals he had witnessed with eccentric winemakers all over the world. Syd described peculiar collections of art collectors who had purchased her work. Amelia shared more of her funny real estate stories about people's outlandish requirements for buying a house. If one classmate hadn't been murdered and another attacked and fighting for her life, it might have been fun.

The reunion photographer continued taking photos throughout dinner and I briefly hoped he would get a chance to eat. Amelia and Bo got up to give a rather amusing presentation of photos from the yearbook. Amelia had been awful to me during high school but it did seem like she was a much nicer adult.

Marco was upset that he couldn't attend Ricky's presentation and wanted to set up a day to meet and talk about how they could use Ricky's proprietary game system to promote Marco's import business. As they chatted away, Chance, who was sitting on my other side, leaned in and asked, "Penny for your thoughts?"

I started and realized I had been staring off into the distance at nothing. I sighed. "No thoughts really. I was just thinking about Sunny and hoping the surgery went well."

Chance laid his arm along the back of my chair and gently rubbed my back. "I'm sure she'll pull through. She's a fighter. Remember back in high school when she fell off the cheerleader pyramid? She got right back up and finished the game even though she had to wear a cast for the next two months."

"This weekend is so surreal. MJ was killed and Sunny attacked. Do you think it was the same attacker for both of them?

Chance continued rubbing my back, which was beginning to send tingles down my spine. "I'm sure the police will figure something out soon. Ty is a smart guy."

I agreed and mentally shook my head. "Look, the band is changing over for the dancing part of the evening. Let's see if the photographer can get a good group shot of us," I waved at the table, "instead of all those candid ones with my mouth full of food or hanging open in shock."

Chance pushed back from the table to go find the photographer as Amelia came back and sat down.

Ricky looked around. "Where's Bo?"

Amelia looked a bit concerned. "I think the stress of all the reunion planning has gotten to him. He said he had a headache and was going back to the room to take some aspirin."

I thought it might be the stress of keeping old secrets, but I didn't share that with Amelia. Chance returned with the photographer and we all stood together for a group photo. The photographer told us that it would be on display tomorrow during the ice cream social if we wanted to buy a copy.

We heard caustic laughter from a nearby table. Amelia glanced over and a disgusted look washed over her face. "That woman is so irritating. She thinks she's the mayor, not Brad."

I looked in the same direction and saw Shannon monopolizing the conversation at her table. Mindy and some people I didn't recognize were listening raptly. Julian, as always, was tapping away at his phone, while Mayor Brad looked at it longingly.

Amelia shuddered. "She always wants to get together with me and Rob...Bo," she smiled, conceding defeat. "Frankly, I'm running out of excuses."

Syd leaned in confidentially. "I thought you were all friends."

Amelia scoffed and whispered loudly. "Not in a million years. All she ever talks about is Brad's future in politics and what they should and shouldn't do." She looked over quickly again. "I hope he does get elected to another office so they move away from Harmony."

Everyone at the table chuckled and ducked down as Shannon gazed over at our table. Shannon whispered something to Mayor Brad and got up. She walked by our table, looked at all the empty wine bottles, sighed loudly as if we were all a disappointment to her, and continued walking. As soon as she was past, our laughter became uncontrollable and Syd was gasping for air.

The music finally started playing and everyone got up and started dancing in groups. The band played all covers from the year 2000 and our whole table was having fun. Cal Jr. said goodnight and left around 10:30, telling the group that he maintained a strict bedtime schedule to keep himself healthy and fit. Syd rolled her eyes and pulled me back out to the dance floor. I was exhausted by the time they called the last song so I begged off and sank into my chair. I grabbed my glass of water and held it up to my forehead to help me cool off. Syd joined me a minute later and drank some water as well.

As the music ended, everyone staggered back to the table. Marco was the only one who still looked energized. He was still bopping in rhythm with the last song that had played.

"Where are we going for after-hours tonight?" he asked. "Back to your suite?"

Ricky looked hopeful but Syd was shaking her head emphatically. "No way. Ty will be super pissed off if we host another party tonight."

I added, "Plus, I'm really tired. I'm not used to late nights anymore and I do not want to be hung over tomorrow."

Marco just shook his head. "Well, I'm off to find a party if anyone wants to join me?" He looked around and Ricky nodded enthusiastically. "Okay, let's go see what trouble two young men on the prowl can get into."

I laughed as the two of them nearly skipped out of the room. I looked at Chance who was yawning loudly. I snickered at him. "How are you going to run a bar if you can't stay awake past 11:30?"

Chance quickly silenced his yawn. "I'll have to build up the stamina." He grinned. "Or hire a night manager." The room had almost cleared out now. He stood up and bowed solemnly. "Ladies, may I escort you upstairs?"

If only he had an English accent, I thought.

Syd giggled. "That would be most gentlemanly, kind sir."

Amelia looked at her watch. "I'm fine. I'll see you at breakfast tomorrow. I need to go over some final details for the last few events." She waved as she walked off toward the exit.

Chapter Twenty-Six

Syd, Chance, and I made our way out of the ballroom and joined the queue for the two elevators. I wondered where Marco and Ricky had gone but figured Ricky was certainly capable of finding his own way back to the room. Every time an elevator door would open, people would shuffle in and the line would stop until the next elevator came along. Even though the wait seemed endless, the party atmosphere continued and we chatted with various classmates as we waited for our turn. We finally moved to the front of the line, the elevator door opened, and I stepped in with a few other people. Suddenly, Syd and Chance were shoved back as a boisterous, drunken group from one of the other events at the hotel pushed their way onto the elevator and filled it up. The door closed on an astonished Syd as I waved and mouthed "See you upstairs."

As the elevator ascended, people got off on every floor. Every single floor. Finally, I was the last person on the elevator as I was apparently the only special one on the penthouse level. I got off the elevator and made my way down the eerily quiet hallway. The police had cleared out already, leaving only traces of fingerprint dust on walls and door jambs. There didn't seem to be a police officer on guard on every floor tonight. I walked quietly down the hall and saw one of the guest room doors was open wide. I slowed down as I approached it and noticed that the room was pitch black inside. I had no idea whose room this was, or even if they were part of the reunion.

I fought with myself for a moment as to whether I should investigate and then smartly decided to go back to the elevator bank and wait for Syd to come up. As I turned around and headed back, I thought I could hear the sound of the elevator moving up toward my floor already, but it was probably stopping at every single floor as well. Then I heard a blood-curdling scream and dropped to the ground as a figure dressed entirely in black with their face covered with a balaclava came running up to me. The person kicked me twice in the side and screeched "Mind your own business!" just as the elevator dinged and Syd and Chance got off.

The assailant turned and ran in the other direction but not before I kicked the person's left foot as hard as I could and the person stumbled. That will leave a mark, I thought with confidence. Syd and Chance flew up the hallway and dropped to their knees beside me. I registered the sound of the stairway door opening and then felt Syd and Chance's hands on me.

"Kat! Kat! Are you okay?" Syd screamed.

I sat up slowly and gingerly touched my side. "I think I'm fine, but I think the killer may have been waiting for me." I pointed to the open guest room. Chance stood up and approached the open door with his fists in front of him like a boxer. He leaned in and called out, "Hello? Is anyone in here? Your door is open!"

He didn't hear a sound so he used his elbow to turn on a light. "Oh, crap," he exclaimed softly.

Syd helped me to my feet and winced as I made a groaning noise and had trouble straightening up. "What is it, Chance?" Syd shouted to him. "What do you see?"

Chance went into the room and we could hear him moving about as I limped toward the door with Syd's help. We peered in and saw Chance bent over behind one of the sofas. He straightened up and looked at me and Syd.

"Syd, call Ty." He looked back down at the floor as Syd and I carefully made our way into the room. We looked at the floor and gasped as Chance shook his head. "It's Bo. He's dead."

I was not surprised to see a steak knife sticking out of Bo's chest or the pool of blood spilling across the floor. I pulled my phone out and dialed 9-1-1 as Syd phoned Ty.

"We should wait outside for the police," I instructed. I turned to head back to the hallway and stumbled over the searing pain in my side.

"Are you okay?" Chance inquired with genuine concern in his voice.

I shook my head. "The killer kicked me right on one of my stab wounds. It really hurts!"

Chance slipped his arm around me, being careful to not touch my sore side. He helped me out into the hallway as I made the call to 9-1-1. Syd followed us out and stood nearby. Chance slipped his other arm around Syd and the three of us huddled together until we heard the elevator's tone and the sound of running feet in the stairway.

Help had arrived.

Chapter Twenty-Seven

Ty was pacing the length of the living room in our suite, speaking on the phone with the State Police and replying with a bunch of "yes, sirs." He finally hung up and turned to glare at me, Syd, and Chance.

"I thought I told you two to stay together?" he demanded, ignoring Chance.

Syd jumped up from the couch. "We were together. All night. We got separated at the elevator by a bunch of drunks jumping on and knocking me and Chance out of the way."

He made a grunting noise and skewered me with a glower. "I thought I told you not to find any more dead bodies?"

Chance groaned. "Come on, Ty. It's not like she was looking for a dead body."

I chimed in simultaneously. "Geez, Ty. It wasn't my fault. It's not like I wanted to find another dead body – the body of someone I just ate dinner with!"

Ty rubbed at his face hard. "I know. I'm sorry. There's just no evidence." He sank onto the couch next to me.

"Go through it one more time for me, please."

I took a deep breath and quipped. "Third time's a charm?"

Ty took out his notebook so he could review his notes while he listened to me. "I'm hoping you remember a tiny detail, like a better description than a person dressed all in black with a black balaclava covering their face."

I angrily tried to stand up but winced from the pain and sunk back onto the cushions. Syd and Chance both leaned in and each put an arm around me. Ty waved at the deputy by the door to hurry the paramedics.

The deputy ducked outside and when he stepped back in, he raised two fingers. I sighed and launched my story. Again.

After finishing all I could remember, I added, "I'm sorry I don't have a better description of the killer, Ty. As soon as I heard screaming, I dropped to the floor. I'm unarmed and," I pointed at my side, "still not recovered from the stab wounds. I knew I couldn't fight."

Ty nodded. "Okay, so the 'assailant' (said with air quotes) was of ordinary height, dressed all in black with a," he consulted his notes, "balaclava covering most of their head. You can't say if they were tall or short, fat or skinny, black or white, or any other details?"

I retorted angrily, "You get down on the ground, curl up in a ball, and tell me what details you notice about who is kicking you in the side."

Syd piped up and looked at Chance. "We only saw the person as they were running away. No idea of any more details than Kat provided."

Chance nodded. "I can't even tell you if the person was taller than me or not. By the time we got to Kat, they were at the far end of the hall." He looked at me tenderly. "All we cared about at that moment was making sure Kat was okay."

Ty held his hands up in defeat. "You're right. I'm sorry. I'm just frustrated." He looked at us again. "Piss anyone off lately?"

I was about to reply angrily then deflated a little. "Well, I was threatened twice during dinner tonight."

Syd and I recounted Shannon's odd behavior and Mindy's overt threat in the ladies' room. Ty wrote their names down in his notebook and rolled his eyes. "Great. I get to speak to the Mayor's wife and Mindy Vanderbilt. This night just keeps getting better and better."

Syd leaned into him and gave him a hug. "You'll figure it all out, honey. I know you will."

Ty kissed the top of Syd's head as the paramedics came in and looked to see who they needed to check. I meekly raised my hand and they asked me what was wrong. I told them about being kicked where I had an earlier injury from a stab wound. They consulted briefly and decided it would be best to bring me to the hospital to have an X-ray. They strapped me onto a stretcher and wheeled me out. Syd and Chance were by my side as Ricky came down the hall toward our suite.

Ricky looked at me, all the police clustered in the hallway outside Bo's room, and then at Ty.

"Not another one," he asked.

Ty nodded grimly and went to go join his officers down the hall. Ricky turned and jogged after my little entourage of friends and EMTs, catching up to us as the elevator opened. "I'm not staying here by myself." As we got downstairs, it looked like Marco was finishing up being interviewed by a detective.

As the paramedics wheeled me to the ambulance, they were adamant that my friends couldn't ride with me, despite Syd's heated objections. I saw Marco hold up his car keys as I was loaded in and pointed him out to Syd. As the ambulance doors closed, I could see my friends silently headed across the parking lot toward Marco.

Chapter Twenty-Eight

Fortunately, the Emergency Room was quiet. They took me in for x-rays and I was out within two hours with a fistful of painkillers and an admonition to take it easy for a week. My four friends jumped up to greet me as the ER staff wheeled me out and I started to cry at the sight of them. I swiped at my tears and they each gave me a half hug.

It was after 2:30 a.m. and we all piled into Marco's van – Chance teased him mercilessly about having a minivan but Marco said it was for local wine deliveries – and headed back to the resort. Marco claimed that he had a Tesla sedan at his house but Chance said he didn't believe him. Marco started driving down High Street. Chance told him he was going the wrong way and Marco replied, "Not the wrong way for McDonald's." Chance groaned and Marco replied indignantly. "Dinner was more than six hours ago and I'm starving after all that dancing." He looked at everyone's tired faces and grinned, "Plus, I don't think anyone of us will be getting up for breakfast tomorrow morning."

Marco pulled into the drive-thru and didn't even ask anyone what they wanted. He ordered what sounded like enough food for ten people. After we picked it up at the window, Marco pulled to a parking spot and started handing food out randomly to everyone. It looked like way too much food, but we polished it all off.

Syd let out a little burp and started giggling. "I guess I was hungry, too."

Everyone agreed and then promptly started yawning again. Chance got out to dump all the trash and then we headed back to the resort, which was quiet at this time of the night, or rather, morning.

After Marco parked, we trudged into the lobby in a bedraggled walk of shame. I heard crying from behind a pillar and peeked around to see Amelia sitting by herself, weeping. Syd and I looked at each other and then walked over and sat down on the couch next to Amelia.

I took a breath. "We're so sorry about Bo, Amelia. Is there anything we can do for you?"

Amelia put her hands to her face and burst into a fresh bout of tears.

"What are you doing here all by yourself?" asked Syd, rubbing Amelia's back.

"I didn't know where to go." She looked at them with tears running down her face. "I certainly couldn't go back to that room and the hotel is fully booked. I couldn't even go home as Bo has, or had, the house keys."

I looked at Syd over Amelia's bent head as she started sobbing again and we made a silent agreement.

I asked her gently, "Amelia, we have a two-bedroom suite. Please come up to our room. We can find you something to wear and the hotel will have amenities for you."

Amelia looked at us hopefully. "Are you sure? I won't be putting you out?"

"Of course not. Syd and I can share one of the bedrooms and Ricky was sleeping on the pull-out sofa anyway."

Ricky came forward and knelt in front of Amelia. "Please come. We really want you to."

Amelia nodded and let us lead her to the elevator. Ricky stopped at the front desk and got an amenities kit for Amelia. When we got off the elevator and walked by Amelia and Bo's room, Marco and Chance formed a small barrier so Amelia wouldn't see the crime scene tape and the deputy guarding the door. We all noticed the police and forensics teams packing up their gear.

When we got closer to our suite, Officer Freely was standing outside our door and reassured us that she would remain there until morning. Marco and Chance escorted us into the room and Marco pulled out a McDonald's bag that he had been hiding in his jacket and handed it to Amelia.

"In case you're hungry…"

Ricky looked at him indignantly. "You were holding out?"

Marco grinned. "I thought I might want a late, er, later night snack."

Amelia took the bag and thanked Marco. Her eyes started filling with tears again so Marco and Chance hugged everyone good-bye and left for their own rooms. We all, except for Amelia, said we would try to make it down for the club meetups at 9:30. Ricky asked if there was anything he could do for us and then went to get ready for bed when we said we were all fine and planning on going straight to sleep.

Syd and I got Amelia settled in the bedroom I had been using. It had a private bathroom and a king-sized bed. Fortunately, Syd's room had two queens. Amelia grabbed each of our hands and looked us each in the eye. Her eyes were still brimming with tears, but she sniffled and said sincerely, "Thank you both so much. I really appreciate your kindness, especially…" she trailed off and looked away. She looked back at us and took a deep breath. Her words tumbled out, "Especially because I was such a bitch to both of you in high school." She shook her head. "I don't know why I did it but I was horrible and mean and I wouldn't blame either of you if you had left me down in that lobby."

I remembered Bo telling me how Amelia was trying to make amends and thought there was no greater proof than this heartfelt show of gratitude. I leaned in and hugged Amelia. "The past is the past. Let's start fresh moving forward."

Syd was now sniffling, too. "Yeah, Amelia. Let's just start fresh," and she leaned in to hug Amelia, too. We stayed like that for a minute until we broke apart, a little embarrassed, and Amelia looked over at the bag of food I had set near the television.

"I think I'm going to eat that food that Marco gave me. McDonald's has always been my guilty pleasure."

Syd and I smiled at her, swiping at the tears on our faces. Syd grinned, "Right? It tastes so good!"

I made a disgusted face. "McDonald's? That's gross!" The other two looked at me with shame etched across their faces. I continued. "I prefer Wendy's." This made us all smile and Syd and I closed the door to give Amelia some privacy.

Ricky was setting up his sofa bed and stretching out the kinks that had built up in his back and neck. "Are we really going to the club meetups tomorrow at 9:30?"

I nodded firmly. "Yes. We need to talk to our suspects again and see if anyone gives anything away."

Syd looked at me in disbelief. "Kat! You promised Ty you would leave the investigation to the police."

I nodded somberly. "And so I am. I'm just going to talk to our suspects."

Ricky climbed onto the sofa bed and sat staring at us. "Suspects? Have you narrowed the field?"

I yawned. "I think so," I yawned again. "Can we go over it tomorrow morning though? I'm about to fall asleep on my feet and it's already almost 4:00 a.m."

Ricky nodded and Syd turned and walked into the second bedroom. I followed and brushed my teeth while Syd used the separate toilet facilities. We switched positions and then we both fell into separate beds. I think I fell asleep before I even had a chance to reply to Syd's "good night."

Chapter Twenty-Nine

Syd, Ricky, and I ordered room service on Sunday morning and even then, we couldn't stop yawning. Amelia had yet to emerge from the bedroom and I thought it would be best to let her sleep.

I stretched my arms over my head and heard crackling sounds throughout my body. Suddenly, I doubled over and grabbed my side.

Ricky shook his head and leaned in to pour another cup of coffee. "Did you forget your little trip to the ER last night? You will probably be sore for a few days." He leaned back and looked at me sharply. "Not that I'm letting you use that as an excuse. You will be coming to the gym with me for our free membership next week."

I slowly straightened up and gingerly touched my side. I growled at Ricky, "That remains to be seen."

Ricky smiled. "Cal Jr. won't let you back out."

I looked sharply at Ricky. "What do you mean?"

Ricky slapped his head. "Ah, I forgot! I never told you what I found out last night when Marco and I went looking for some after-hours parties."

Syd made an impatient motion with her hands.

"Cal Jr. was at one of them. I guess his body *isn't* his temple. I told him again how excited I was for the membership and he asked me if you would definitely be coming with me." Ricky leaned in confidentially. "I think he wants to ask you out, Kat."

I shuddered. "No, thank you."

Ricky snickered. "Okay, but you may be missing out on a mint."

Syd looked at him quizzically. "What do you mean? Is the gym making that much money?" She rubbed her hands together greedily and smiled slyly, "Maybe I should leave Ty for Cal Jr." Then she shuddered, too.

Ricky shook his head. "No, but he told me privately that he plans to franchise The Mercury. He said he had to leave dinner early Friday night to meet with three franchise specialists on what needed to be done. They met with him at O'Reilly's Irish Pub and he got back just in time to see the ambulance taking MJ's body away." He chuckled. "He also said he had to deal with his drunk and freaked out father, so he put a towel down on his passenger seat and drove him home. Left him with his mother to deal with."

I thought for a moment. "Very compassionate, eh? I guess I can scratch him off my suspect list then."

Syd scrunched up her face. "Why?"

"Well, if he left before dinner was over and didn't get back until after MJ had died, he couldn't have killed her." I thought again. "I definitely saw MJ going into the lounge for drinks after dinner."

The second bedroom door slowly opened and Amelia came out in one of the hotel robes. Her eyes were puffy and bloodshot and her face was gaunt and haggard. Syd, Ricky, and I instantly stopped talking and watched her cross the room toward us. Ricky got up to bring another chair over for her and Syd poured her a cup of coffee. She sighed deeply, took a large gulp of coffee, and looked at us imploringly.

"Please don't stop talking on my account. I'm sure that will happen enough in the coming days."

Syd walked around the table and bent to put her arm around Amelia. "I wish this had never happened but as you know, it's bound to get worse before it gets better."

Ricky hissed, "Syd!"

Syd rubbed Amelia's back a little more and turned her attention to Ricky. "What? She's not stupid. I don't want to lie to her."

Amelia squeezed Syd's hand and smiled kindly at Ricky. "It's okay. The next few days are going to be awful; I know." She looked around the table. "Did I hear you three talking about Cal Jr.? Is he a suspect?"

Chapter Thirty

Ricky jumped in. "We can change the subject." He shot daggers at me and Syd. "What would you like to talk about, Amelia?"

"I'd like to continue talking about suspects, motives, and alibis. I need to know why someone killed MJ and Bo and tried to kill Sunny. Or maybe did kill Sunny. We still don't know how she's doing, do we?"

Syd squeezed her hand. "We can do this later. You don't want to talk about this now."

Amelia put down the coffee mug forcefully. "I *do* want to talk about it, right now! My husband is dead, and the same person probably killed the others too—or tried to. I want to know who and why!"

Syd studied her thoughtfully. "If you're certain...?"

"I am," Amelia retorted. "Let's get started."

I chewed my lip and stared at my Coke. "Amelia, do you know of any reason that anyone would want to kill B...Robert?"

Amelia sniffed. "You can call him Bo. That's how he always referred to himself." She shook her head slowly. "No. Everybody liked Bo. He was a good boss, a great father, and a genuinely nice guy."

I gazed at her. "How about from back in high school? Would anyone hold a grudge?"

Amelia sighed. "I suppose you're talking about all those old rumors about something happening to a girl in the locker room." She sat up a little straighter. "I can assure you that Bo did not drug or rape anyone." She paused, then deflated a little, and sagged back against the chair... "That's not entirely the truth," she whispered softly.

Syd, Ricky, and I all gaped at her and Syd opened her mouth to speak. Amelia put her hands up quickly. "No, no, no. That's not what I meant." She took a ragged breath. "When Ned Anders came back to

Harmony and took over as pastor of our church, Bo started having nightmares." She examined her folded hands. "That's when he confessed to me about the incident with S-S-Sunny." She looked up at them. "Not that he had participated, mind you, but he did see the recording afterward and never did anything about it." She took a deep breath. "Seeing Ned after all those years brought the memories back to the surface and he was absolutely torn up about it."

I bristled, "Not as badly as Sunny, I'm sure."

Amelia's hands flew to her face. "Oh my, no! I don't mean to imply that at all." She fell back against the chair again. "I'm sure Sunny never got over it. How could she?"

I regarded Amelia wearily. "Why did Ned bring these memories back? Just because he was on the football team, too?"

Amelia looked flatly at me. "Cal Jr. and Ned were both there when the, uhm, when *it* happened. According to Ned, Cal Jr. slipped the drug into her drink. Ned made the recording, but Brad showed it around to the other guys. Plus, Cal Jr. was caught on the video."

Syd sat back and let out the breath she had been holding. "Great, another suspect."

Amelia looked at each of us in turn. "You have suspects?"

I felt chagrined. "Not exactly, but we have collected some information over the weekend that ties the past to the present and everything that's happened." I stared intently at Amelia. "Who raped her, Amelia? Who could do something like that?"

Amelia wrung her hands. "It would ruin his life and his future if it got out."

"Maybe his life needs to be ruined if he could do that to someone," I snapped back, furious.

Amelia gazed out the window at the sunny day. "Bo went and spoke to Ned one night at the rectory and they talked for hours. Ned confessed how guilty he had felt about that, um, incident, his whole life. Before he was ordained, he had come to Harmony to throw himself at Sunny's mercy. He told her he was willing to go to the police and confess to his part if she wanted and told her how very sorry he was about what had happened to her." A brief smile flitted across her face. "Ned told Bo that they both cried and Sunny told him that she forgave him. She also said how much she appreciated the apology and wished Ned well on his spiritual journey."

I interjected. "They seemed to be getting along okay at our after-hours on Friday night."

Amelia genuinely smiled. "Yes. When he moved back to Harmony a few years after that, he looked her up again and invited her to attend his services. They became friends."

Ricky blurted out. "What about Bo? Did he talk to Sunny?"

Amelia nodded. "Yes. After speaking with Ned at the rectory, Bo went looking for Sunny the next day at the bakery. He sat down with her and apologized for doing nothing to help her after seeing that video." Amelia sighed again. "Sunny told Bo that she forgave him. She said they were all just basically kids at the time and nobody knew what to do, even her. She thanked him for his apology, however, and his nightmares started to go away."

I stood up quickly and knocked my chair over. "I'm glad everyone who *didn't* rape Sunny apologized to her and she forgave them." I leaned over Amelia. "Who. Raped. Sunny?"

Amelia wrung her hands a bit more and stared into her coffee mug. She looked up and blinked her tears away. "It was Brad and Cal Jr."

"Mayor Brad?" Syd and Ricky asked incredulously.

138

"Yes. Sunny used to hang out with them and Ned, and I think she had a crush on Brad."

I pictured what Brad looked like now and grimaced.

Amelia saw my expression. "Don't think of him now. Remember him back in high school. He was good looking back then and a football player. Not like now." I sunk back into my seat.

Amelia started to run her hands through her hair but stopped when they got stuck in the tangled mess. Amelia said, "I dated him for a while in high school." I shuddered. "I'm lucky he didn't pull this stunt on me. Not that I want him to have pulled it on anyone." She sighed again. "Brad got hold of the Rohypnol and told Cal how much to put in her drink. Cal couldn't have figured that out on his own."

"What about Ned? I can't believe Sunny could forgive him if he raped her too! And now he's a minister?" I asked her indignantly. Amelia shook her head. "Ned didn't assault her, he just filmed it. Not that that wasn't bad enough."

I exhaled deeply. "Before we try to narrow down our suspect list, where is this person getting all the knives? Are they from the hotel?"

Amelia shook her head. "After both MJ and Sunny were stabbed with knives that are, by the way, the exact same model we use here, Bo had the staff do an inventory. There were no knives missing." She wiped at a tear. "I don't know where they're coming from."

"Okay, then. Let's talk about who we can rule out." I held a finger up in the air. "So, Cal Jr. was bitter about being dumped by MJ after he got her all toned and beautiful but he has an alibi for when MJ was killed. He was meeting with the potential franchisors." I put a second finger up. "It seems like Ned made peace with Sunny, but would he be worried that MJ's book would get him in trouble?"

Amelia shook her head. "No, that book came out years ago. Plus, he has an alibi too. He sat with Stuart and Molly at dinner and they skipped the dancing to have a mini-prayer group in the hotel lobby. A few other classmates joined in as well."

Ricky nodded eagerly. "Right! He showed up at our after-hours with Stuart and Molly."

I put up a third finger. "Sunny may have been disappointed or even angry that MJ had published Sunny's secret, but she certainly didn't stab herself. Of course, there could be more than one killer, but I don't think she would have stabbed MJ anyway."

I put up a fourth finger. "Bo wouldn't have wanted anyone to know about what happened in high school and that he did nothing about it, but Syd had a conversation with him on the way to Ricky's presentation and there wouldn't have been time for him to stab Sunny, get cleaned up, and race back downstairs in that short amount of time." I winced as I looked across at Amelia. "Plus, he was also killed, so that definitely rules him out." Amelia pursed her lips and started to speak but said nothing.

I put up the last finger on that hand. "Mindy."

"Mindy?" Amelia asked, astonished.

I nodded. "Yup. She was furious that MJ seduced and then dumped her little brother. And maybe seeing Bo and you again in this setting brought back all the jealousy and rage? I don't know why she would have been angry at Sunny though."

"Mindy was always mad at everyone for some made up reason or another," Amelia muttered. "She totally ignored MJ in high school, then thought MJ should help her little brother in Hollywood after she became famous." She thought for a second. "She was not happy when they moved in together and she was furious when MJ dumped him." She looked out

140

the window. "She also blamed MJ for Xavier killing himself, though he had been an addict since high school."

Amelia looked out the window. "Mindy was also angry with Sunny because Sunny wouldn't give her the discount she wanted on bakery products for her catering company. She thought that she should get 50 percent off because they went to high school together and Sunny told her 'No,' in no uncertain terms. She would have lost money at that rate." She sighed. "And Bo...well you're right about that; she never forgave him for breaking up with her in high school and dating me. It's been 20 years and she still makes snide comments about how I 'stole him away from her'. And now he's gone..." Amelia broke off and turned her face away, clearly crying. We looked awkwardly at one another, and Syd reached out a hand to touch Amelia's shoulder.

"Damn it!" Amelia slammed her hand down on the table, making us and the coffee cups jump. "It can't be Mindy. Right after dinner on Friday, she got into a huge fight with her husband. She attached herself to me and Bo at the bar and, well," she shrugged, "you saw how drunk she got. She was with us for the whole night."

I looked grimly around the table and raised a sixth finger. "That leaves Mayor Brad."

Syd stared up at the ceiling. "I guess I should call Ty and let him know that we figured it out."

Chapter Thirty-One

As Syd picked up her mobile phone from the table, it rang in her hand and startled her and she dropped it. She picked it up and answered, "Hi, honey. I was just going to call you." She listened for a few seconds. "No, we're up already." She looked around the table. "Well, we're not showered and dressed yet, but you can come in." She got up from the table, walked to the door, and opened it. Ty was standing on the other side with his phone pressed against his ear.

"Hi, honey," he smiled and leaned down to kiss her on the nose.

She pushed him away and regarded him critically. "You look horrible!"

"Thanks, babe." He looked at her bloodshot eyes and knotted hair, then sighed and wisely made no comment as he sat in a chair and poured himself a cup of coffee.

Syd leaned down and put her arm around his shoulders. "I'm sorry. Lack of sleep is making me bitchy."

Ty took a big gulp of coffee and exhaled deeply. "That's okay. I feel horrible, too, if that's any consolation." He rubbed his eyes. "We're getting nowhere fast on this case." He looked apologetically at Amelia. "I'm sorry, Amelia. We will get the person who killed Bo; I just need a few more pieces of the puzzle."

Syd stepped back and looked at her husband apprehensively "Promise you won't be mad?"

Ty glowered at her and then the rest of the table. "What did you all do now?"

Ricky interjected. "Hey, don't be angry, Ty. We solved the case."

Ty jumped up and stared at them. "What?! Didn't I tell you three to butt out and leave it to me?" He looked at Amelia. "Sorry, I'm not angry with you."

Syd stomped her foot and crossed her arms. "Ty Randall! You sit back down and listen to us right now! We did not put ourselves in danger at all but we did talk, and when we put all our information about the past and present together, we came up with the most likely suspect."

Ty sat down warily and leaned forward to rest his elbows on his knees. "Okay, let me have it. Who do you think is the murderer?"

I took a deep breath and spent the next ten minutes briefly outlining everything we had discussed. When I finished, Syd looked him in the eye and pronounced, "And that's why we think the killer is Mayor Brad."

To his credit, Ty had sat quietly and listened to our suspects, motives, and alibis. He nodded occasionally and asked a clarifying question here and there. When I told him about high school Brad drugging and raping Sunny and how MJ had put it in her book, he was enraged and jumped up to pace around the room. When I finished the summary, he poured another cup of coffee and looked out the window, pondering the suppositions and accusations, his weary shoulders sagging.

The four of us watched him closely, afraid to speak. Finally, he shook his head. "I agree that Mayor Brad is the best suspect. He has the most motive to kill MJ and Bo – and try to kill Sunny – but he has an alibi." He sighed.

"What?" yelled Ricky and Syd while Amelia and I stared at him open-mouthed.

"On Friday after dinner, Shannon had a migraine and went up to their room. Brad took advantage of this rare bit of freedom from Shannon and hooked up with one of the cocktail waitresses in the lounge." He shook his head. "It seems she wants an internship at Town Hall and would do anything," he grimaced briefly, "or anyone, to get it. Including Mayor Brad."

Ricky asked hopefully. "Maybe he got her to provide an alibi for him in exchange for the internship?"

"Unfortunately, no. First of all, she was terrified to be interviewed by the police. But more importantly, she wanted to make sure he couldn't back out on his promise so she commemorated the occasion with selfies of the two of them in the boathouse in," he cleared his throat, "various stages of undress." He shuddered. "That is not a picture I can just unsee." He made a disgusted face. "He certainly wanted to make sure he got his money's worth, so to speak, because they hooked up again on Saturday night. I'm not sure where Shannon was then."

Syd frowned. "She probably faked another migraine to get away from Mayor Brad. Maybe she's disgusted by him, too."

Amelia shook her head. "Shannon is totally in love with Brad. Always has been. She is completely invested in Brad becoming a state representative and even governor one day. She loves him, or at least she fakes it really well."

We all sat around the table dejectedly. Amelia looked at her watch and pushed herself back from the table as someone knocked at the door. Ty walked over to answer it.

"I need to get ready for the ice cream social. Any chance of getting into my room for some fresh clothes?" she called to Ty's back.

"This should be Officer Freely now," he called out over his shoulder. "After Syd texted. me last night that you were staying with them, I asked her to choose a few outfits for you and to bring your toiletries." He opened the door and took an evidence bag from the deputy. "We processed the scene early this morning but I still can't let you in."

144

Amelia smiled sadly at Ty. "That's okay. Thank you for that," as she pointed at the bag in Ty's hand.

"Sorry it's an evidence bag. That's all we had."

She nodded grimly and started walking toward the bedroom. Ricky rushed over to her side and put his arm around her. "You don't have to go to the ice cream social, Amelia. Nobody would expect you to." He swept his arm out to include me and Syd. "We can run the event for you. No problem."

"Thanks, I really appreciate the offer, but I think I need the distraction."

Ty watched from the door. "Remember, stay together and let me say this clearly, 'NO. MORE. INVESTIGATING.'"

Syd walked over to him and pushed him gently out the door. "Aye, aye, Captain," she quipped as she saluted him.

Ty gave her an exasperated look and kissed the top of her head as she closed the door behind him.

I jumped up and went running toward the second bedroom. "First dibs on the shower," I called. "We missed the school club reunions, but we still have an ice cream social to attend!"

Syd and Ricky looked at each other and mouthed "Ice cream social?"

"Yup, we've got a killer to catch."

Syd and Ricky sat down and put their heads in their hands.

Chapter Thirty-Two

We met up with Chance and Marco at the ice cream social. Amelia had peeled off to go speak with the resort's event organizers about the end-of-reunion luncheon even though we had also volunteered to help out. Amelia told us she wanted to keep busy or she felt that she would fall apart and that this would also keep her away from her classmates' pitying looks. She assumed that the news had spread through the resort by now.

Chance asked how I was feeling as I limped over to the tent set up outside the tennis courts. Ricky had already gotten a bowl of ice cream and it was loaded with toppings and sauces. Marco looked at him critically.

"What?" Ricky asked around a mouthful of ice cream, chocolate sauce dripping onto his chin.

"You definitely need that gym membership, buddy." He reached over and tweaked Ricky's mid-side. "All that computer work – and that food – is making you soft."

Ricky cringed and then shoved another huge spoonful of the gooey, melting concoction in his mouth. "I'll start eating better as soon as Kat and I activate our membership at The Mercury." He examined me critically. "When do you think you'll feel good enough to start exercising again?"

I shook my head dramatically. "I don't know Ricky. Could be months…"

Ricky looked crestfallen as he carefully swallowed his ice cream, chocolate sauce coating his lips. He sat for a moment and then shrugged. "Guess I'll live it up until then." He smiled and took another huge mouthful of ice cream.

I chuckled. "Not a chance. I'll be good to go within a week, Ricky. No worries."

He looked at his ice cream and then back at me. He hurriedly spooned more ice cream into his mouth.

Chance held up his hands in a halting motion. "Slow down, Ricky. What's the rush?"

Ricky gulped down a bite. "I only have a week to eat what I want. I need to get another bowl before they run out." He turned and went back to the tables set up under the tent. We all laughed and then followed behind him.

After getting our ice cream and toppings, the five of us settled at one of the long rectangular tables set up outside. We huddled together and I quickly brought Chance and Marco up to speed on everything we had learned or deduced, the people with motive we had eliminated, and our current lack of suspects.

Chance and Marco gave each other uneasy looks.

Ricky looked from one to the other. "Spill it, you two!"

Chance shrugged. "It's nothing really. Marco and I went to the scheduled football team meetup this morning." He shrugged. "It was kind of fun seeing everyone but some people have not changed one bit." He grew serious.

I regarded him quizzically. "What do you mean? Who specifically?"

"Cal Jr. is still a pompous ass," huffed Marco. "He was going on and on about franchising The Mercury and how much money he's going to make. All he could talk about was the celebrity endorsements he already had and how he'll be able to hook up with tons of hot young chicks." At Syd's sharp look, he added, "His words, not mine. I find it a repugnant thought."

Chance nodded. "Yeah. Ned seems nice now but he's a little bitter about life in general, especially for a priest." He looked at him a few tables away. "He went through a contentious divorce and barely sees his kids." He looked sad. "I feel bad for him but all he does is complain and doesn't do anything to help himself."

We heard a guffaw of laughter and looked over to see Mayor Brad and Shannon standing with Juan, Stuart, and Molly. Stuart and Molly looked uncomfortable and Juan didn't appear to be paying any attention. Shannon leaned in and whispered in Mayor Brad's ear. He suddenly stopped smiling and fixed his face with an appropriately somber look.

Marco sneered in disgust. "Biggest hypocrite of the whole freaking class."

Chance nodded in agreement.

I looked over at Brad and Shannon, holding hands and – now – looking composed. "Why do you say that?"

Chance took a breath. "He ran for mayor on a campaign of family values, which the town thought was great after the last Mayor ran off with Stan, the butcher's brother." He looked over at Brad again. "At the football meetup, all he did was brag about bagging some gorgeous chick this weekend and how he wasn't going to give her the internship he had promised. He thought it wouldn't look good for his family values image to have a hot young cocktail waitress as his intern." He cleared his throat. "He also told us that being Mayor was good enough for him and he has no intention of running for any other office. Here in Harmony, he has all the perks he wants and loves being treated with respect by the whole town." He shuddered. "He also mentioned all the chicks – again, his word – who want to hook up with the mayor. It was kind of gross."

I looked surprised. "Really? I wonder if his wife knows about any of his extracurricular activities?"

Ricky surreptitiously eyed the couple and made a face. "I doubt it. She looks enraptured by him."

"I don't know," Marco leaned in and whispered, "I heard they've paid off a number of women to maintain Brad's good image."

Syd regarded the couple, "She sure puts up a good front. I guess if she really wants to be a senator or governor's wife, she'll put up with his reprehensible behavior and maybe even help him cover it up." Syd paused as she spied Ty coming out of the hotel with one of his police officers. "I would *definitely* know if Ty was cheating – not that he ever would – and I would NOT put up with it." Ty stopped to have a discussion with one of his officers and pointed down toward the boat house.

Ricky snorted. "He certainly wouldn't live to tell the tale!"

Everyone laughed and nodded, then settled in to eat their ice cream before it melted more. A few minutes later, Shannon came over with Mayor Brad trailing behind her.

Marco stood up and pulled out a chair for Shannon. "Grab some ice cream and have a seat."

Shannon patted her flat stomach and shook her head. "I don't think so. It's too early in the day for dessert." She looked disapprovingly at the five of us with bowls of ice cream sitting in front of us. When her eyes settled on me, she put on a look of concern. "Kat, how are you after last night? Should you even be here?"

I gave Shannon a tight-lipped smile. "I'm fine, Shannon. Thank you for asking. I survived worse in the army."

Shannon nodded sympathetically. "I'm glad you're okay. I was worried when I heard what happened."

I looked at her questioningly. "How did you hear, Shannon? It was the middle of the night and nobody was around. We didn't get back until almost 4 a.m."

Shannon cocked her head to one side. "I was with Brad when he got an update from Chief Randall." She smiled at Syd. "Ty."

Mayor Brad slowly shook his head. "You weren't with me when Ty brought me up to speed. I, uhm," he faltered and glanced quickly at Chance and Marco, "took a walk down to the boathouse this morning and was on my way back when I ran into Ty." He looked over at Shannon. "You were in the shower when I got back to the room."

Shannon shrugged. "That's right. You told me after I got out of the shower, honey."

Mayor Brad scrunched up his face in confusion. "I don't think so, honey."

Shannon patted his shoulder. "I can tell you had a lot to drink last night, Brad, once I wasn't there to stop you. Friday night, too. I'm sure you've just forgotten what you said. I hope you had fun with the boys this weekend. Those kind of nights will have to stop when you run for state representative."

I caught Mayor Brad subtly roll his eyes.

He must have been feeling a little feisty after his encounters with the waitress because he turned, looked at Shannon, and asked accusingly, "And where were you last night, Shannon? I couldn't find you anywhere."

"You mean after you were done 'interviewing' the potential intern?" Shannon asked menacingly.

"If you didn't always have a migraine, Shannon, maybe I wouldn't need to 'interview' interns," Brad spat out maliciously.

"You've been 'interviewing' since high school, Brad. Was this one at least willing?"

We all gaped at Shannon and she immediately realized she had said too much. She looked down at the ground and took a ragged breath to compose herself. She looked out over the harbor and the town in the distance and murmured, "We will miss living in Harmony though, once Brad gets elected to the state house of representatives. Everyone here has

150

always been so nice and friendly and appreciate all that Brad has done for them."

Marco raised his eyebrows and stage-whispered to Chance, "Especially the interns."

Shannon ignored Marco and stood up abruptly. "Brad, honey, we should go see if we can find Amelia and offer our condolences."

Mayor Brad looked warily at Shannon but lumbered to his feet anyway. "Sure thing." As they walked away, I heard Shannon whisper to Brad, "Then we just have the luncheon and we can put this whole terrible tragedy behind us once and for all."

Mayor Brad nodded meekly and let Shannon take his hand and lead him away.

Chapter Thirty-Three

Marco looked around curiously. "Where *is* Amelia?"

Syd yawned and stood up, gathering the disposable ice cream bowls to throw out. "She wanted to keep herself busy so she went to make sure everything was all set for the luncheon."

Chance stood up. "I don't like the thought of her being all alone," he nodded in the direction Brad and Shannon had walked in, "Especially with those two looking for her. Let's go see if she wants any help now."

Syd replied, "She should be with the resort events people, not alone, but we can go check on her and see if she needs any help with the luncheon."

Ricky agreed. "Yeah, that ice cream just whetted my appetite." He rubbed his stomach. "I wonder what they are going to serve for lunch?"

Marco rolled his eyes. "Wait until Cal Jr. gets you into the gym. You'll start treating your body "like a temple" and won't even dream of eating like this."

Ricky looked skeptically at him. "I notice you ate a bowl of ice cream, too. Not to mention McDonalds last night." Ricky mimed picking up a telephone. "Hello, kettle? This is Marco. You're black." We all roared in laughter at Marco's look of outrage.

"My body has always been a temple. I just cheat sometimes so all the ladies don't think I'm too perfect."

I laughed out loud, then blinked and stared at Marco.

He looked confused. "What?"

"Ladies?" I asked.

Marco huffed. "Yes, ladies." He squinted at her suspiciously. "What are you asking?"

I tried to shrug and stammered out, "S-S-Syd s-s-said you…"

Chance, Ricky, and Syd burst out laughing at my discomfort and Marco's reaction, which made Marco even more indignant and sulky.

Syd merely shrugged and laughed until her shoulders shook.

Chance, still chuckling, put his arm around Marco. "*That* face is going to make me a smile for a long time." He sobered a little when he saw my red face.

"As if we want him on *my* team," taunted Ricky, and Marco became even more disgruntled.

"I can join any team I want," he declared emphatically. "It's 2020. I am a metrosexual who is comfortable with my own," he inclined his head at Ricky, "or anyone else's sexuality." He put on a sad face and fumed to me. "I'm just upset that you haven't noticed that I've been flirting with you all weekend."

Chance looked at me quizzically, my jaw dropped, and I started sweating. I couldn't get any words out. Syd came to my rescue, reminding everyone we were supposed to go find Amanda. I closed my mouth, turned, and fled up the small hill toward the hotel while the others followed along behind me.

I was completely embarrassed that I had basically just called Marco gay – not that there's anything wrong with that. Not that it mattered at all and Marco certainly didn't seem to be insulted personally. Clearly, he wasn't at all homophobic, which was kind of refreshing in a former football player. It was just that I didn't want to be one of those people who assumed anything about anyone. I stopped and stood rigid for a moment. Wait! Did Marco just say that he had been flirting with me all weekend? How did I feel about that? What about Chance? Hadn't he been flirting with me, too? Was I part of some old high school competition? I shook my head. Whoa! Now you think that two of the most eligible bachelors to ever graduate from Harmony High are interested in you? Like you're some prize? (Damn! The questions are back!) I needed to get over myself.

Damn that Syd! All of this was her fault. I vowed to get her back after all this was over. I heard them noisily coming along behind me and I resumed my mad rush through the resort, trying to get some distance. My face was still flaming red in embarrassment.

I made my way through the empty dining room headed toward the kitchen. I glanced out a window and my eye was caught by Mayor Brad, perched on one of the chaise lounges by the pool and grabbing at one of the waitresses who was frantically trying to stay out of his reach. There were a few men around him and they were all laughing at the poor woman's misfortune. I briefly wondered if she was the woman who wanted the internship and then I flashed to Shannon saying they were going to find Amelia to pay their respects. Why was Mayor Brad by himself? Where was Shannon?

Chapter Thirty-Four

As I entered through the swinging doors into the kitchen, I heard a scuffling noise and heavy breathing. I looked frantically around and saw Shannon advancing on Amelia, who was kneeling on the ground with a big, bloody gash on her forearm. With her good arm, she was frantically reaching around on the counter, trying to find something to defend herself with. Damn it! I realized Shannon was threatening Amelia with a steak knife that looked identical to the ones that had been used on MJ, Bo, and Sunny. Where was she getting all these knives?

Something clicked, and I remembered a conversation earlier in the weekend where somebody had mentioned that Mayor Brad sold premium cutlery before he was elected mayor. Crap! The two of them probably had boxes of knives at home. How many people would Shannon kill before they ran out?

I mentally and physically shook myself to focus on the situation in front of me. I took a calming breath and watched Shannon get closer to Amelia. She was so focused on Amelia that she hadn't heard me come in. I looked around the kitchen, searching for something heavy or pointy to get Shannon away from Amelia. I tiptoed past the sinks to one of the stoves. I was proud of myself for being so stealthy, until my side spasmed and I knocked over a garbage can.

Shannon chuckled mirthlessly. "I hear you back there, Kitty Kat. You won't find any weapons in here and I know you don't carry a gun anymore. I was worried about that yesterday when I tripped over you in the hallway after getting rid of Bo and his big blabbermouth."

Until that instant, I hadn't really believed that Shannon could be the killer. She sounded very composed and relaxed – despite brandishing a steak knife in Amelia's direction. I looked around frantically, trying to find something to throw or hit her with. The kitchen was impeccably spotless with everything put away. Damn that dedicated kitchen staff!

"Shannon, wait. Amelia never did anything to you. Why are you doing this?"

Shannon glanced over her shoulder at me for a second and scoffed. "Don't patronize me, Kat. I know you've been snooping around all weekend and you've found out about Brad and his little indiscretion in high school. Everyone always thinks they're so superior." She lost her composure for a moment and sniffled. "Do you think I don't hear the whispers?" She turned to glare at Amelia. "She and Mindy think they are so much better than everyone else with their giant houses and all their money. Well, Brad's going places. He is. He's going to be a Very Important Man someday as long as," she faltered, "well, as long as the voters in this state never find out about that small mistake in his past."

Small mistake? He raped someone. Worse, he *drugged* and raped someone. The fact that he used the drug meant it was premeditated. Then he had it recorded and distributed. I would spend my last breath making sure that the voters of this state knew everything that Brad did back in high school.

Focus, I told myself grimly. Got to save Amelia first... and myself. "I think Brad would make a great state representative or even governor," I told Shannon earnestly. "I've spent a lot of time with you both this weekend, and I think he's got what it takes, and he really cares about people, I can tell." I eyed Amelia, who had tears streaming down her face and both hands up in a defensive posture as Shannon menaced her with the knife less than two feet away. "Amelia and I don't care about the past, do we, Amelia? We only care about what Brad can do in the future, for our future, for the whole state. I'm sure he'll do great things."

156

Amelia took a shaky breath and stuttered fearfully, "I d-d-don't care about wh-wh-what happ-p-pened in the p-past, Shannon." She looked at me, then under the prep table, and back to me, clearly trying to direct my attention to something, but I couldn't see anything that would help. "H-he has my vote," she declared firmly.

I had used the time that Shannon was focused on Amelia to close the gap until there was only a couple of yards between us. Shannon suddenly spun around, waving the knife at me. She sneered at me. "Oh, really? You two don't care about the past?" She looked at my hand pressed to my side to sooth the spasms. "What if you ever got your hands on the guy who stabbed you? Would you be willing to look the other way?"

I felt my insides turn to ice and my resolve harden. I took a menacing step toward Shannon, my fists balled. "Personal retribution is a different thing," I ground out between my gritted teeth. "That meth head took my life and my future away. He will pay if I ever get my hands on him."

Shannon lunged at me and forced me to step back. She tilted her head back at Amelia who I could see crawling toward the prep table, three feet away, while Shannon had her back turned. "You think she won't find my killing Bo, big dumb Bo, a reason for personal retribution?"

I heard some noises on the other side of the swinging doors behind me. "Why *did* you kill Bo, Shannon? In fact, why kill Marla Jean and attack Sunny and me?"

"You just keep showing up in the wrong place at the wrong time, Kat. Not that I wouldn't like to wipe that smug arrogant smile off your face. Now, however, you know too much." She glanced back at Amelia, who froze on the floor. "Sunny," she spat out, "told MJ that my Brad and his friends drugged and raped her in high school." She made a sound of disbelief. "Like Brad ever had to drug anyone to have sex with him. He's

157

always been a ladies' man. He still is." Her eyes clouded over momentarily and I had to fight back the urge to gag. "Sunny had to go before she could tell that lie to anyone else and ruin Brad's future in politics." She looked wild-eyed at me. "Marla Jean found out about the incident and then," Shannon shook the knife, "She actually had the audacity to write lies about it in her book. She made it sound like Brad forced himself on Sunny. But Brad told me what really happened."

"What really happened, Shannon?" I probed, playing along.

"He told me how they were partying together and how Sunny suggested a foursome. Brad agreed only if he could go first. Ned and Cal Jr. could have sloppy seconds and thirds. He told me that Sunny had been drinking and took a pill and was a little out of it, but that she had asked them to have sex with her before that, so they did." She added mockingly, "Not Father Ned, though. He couldn't get it up. Lame then. Lame now."

I gritted my teeth. "Does that really sound reasonable, Shannon? Do you think any girl back in high school would have wanted to have sex with three guys at once?"

Shannon had tears streaming down her face. "That's just the type of girl Sunny was. She was a whore and now she wants to ruin Brad's life!"

I shook my head emphatically. "No, Shannon. Sunny didn't want Brad. Nobody wants Brad. In fact, he's still manipulating women with lies for sexual favors." I tried using a calm voice. "Sunny was drugged, Shannon. She didn't have a choice in what happened to her."

"You take that back, Kat! You're wrong." She swiped at the tears dripping from her eyes and sniffled, pointing the knife at me. "That's just your opinion, Kat. I remember when you babysat me. You talked about Brad with your friends and other guys on the football team." She continued crying, a big, ugly cry. "I was so jealous." She looked me straight in the

158

eye. "I ALWAYS planned on marrying Brad and having the perfect life. From when I first saw him when I was ten years old." She took a shaky breath and glared at me. "I've been watching you all weekend, Kat. Even now you can't take your eyes off of Brad."

I coughed so I wouldn't laugh. "I was just trying to figure things out, Shannon. I know I could never compete with you for Brad. You two belong together."

Shannon was crying so hard now that I could barely decipher her words. "We do belong together. We always have." She lowered the knife a little and looked at her wedding ring. "Why aren't I enough for him, Kat? Why does he cheat on me?"

Now I'm supposed to provide marriage counseling? I thought. But I had to buy time and keep Shannon's focus on me. "I don't know, Shannon, and it's just terrible. But it's obvious how much he loves you. No one could ever take him away from you."

Out of the corner of my eye, I saw Amelia reach the prep table and stretch her arm underneath. Unfortunately, the closest arm was the one with all the blood on it and she was having a difficult time reaching whatever she wanted under there. The bleeding gash scraped against the side of the prep table and Amelia whimpered audibly.

Shannon wheeled back around to face Amelia, tears and snot flinging everywhere. "What are you doing under there?" she bellowed and took two steps closer to Amelia, who froze in place. Shannon took a deep breath and her tears immediately stopped. She nodded, more to herself than to Amelia or me. "It will be okay, though. Everything will be back on track." She glared down at Amelia. "I didn't know that Bo knew anything until I overheard him telling Syd that he had seen the video – he had to go! Now I need to figure out who else knows." She looked between me and Amelia. "You both understand, right?"

Amelia started sobbing and repeating, "No, no, no…" She dragged her arm across her eyes to wipe away the tears but unfortunately, it was the arm with the gash and she smeared blood across her face.

Shannon faltered and then regarded me plaintively. "You understand, Kat. Right?"

"The whole football team watched that video, Shannon. Are you going to kill them all?"

"If I have to," she wailed.

I was shaking in frustration and fear. Where was everyone? I thought they had been right behind me. Why weren't there people in the kitchen preparing for lunch? Damn it! I slowly swiveled my head, searching for anything to defend myself with.

"I *don't* understand, Shannon. Even if everyone knew, the worst that could have happened is Brad would have been voted out of office. He would not have been elected. The statute of limitations for rape in Massachusetts is fifteen years. He wouldn't even be arrested."

"But his political career would be over! He would have to go back to selling forks, and spoons, and knives…" She glanced at the knife in her hand and stood up a little straighter. "Like this knife. We have boxes of them at home." She took another breath and started composing herself. "You two have to go. With you two gone, nobody will ever connect the deaths to Brad or me."

Suddenly, the swinging door to the dining room crashed open and Syd, Ricky, Marco, and Chance rushed to stand near me. I noticed that Syd had a vase from one of the hall tables with some water still sloshing around inside. Marco had a full wine bottle – seriously, did bottles appear out of thin air when he snapped his fingers? Ricky was holding a serving tray. Chance was not armed, but his mere presence made me feel more secure.

Syd said shakily, "I know, too, Shannon. Are you going to kill me?"

Chance stepped forward, "Me, too. Are you going to kill me?"

Marco sighed, "And me?" And then he waved the wine bottle around like an epée in a sword fight.

Ricky's voice squeaked out, "What about me?"

Shannon looked at all of us and then at the knife in her hand. She burst into tears again and sank to the floor, dropping the knife. It clanked away from her and I quickly kicked it back toward the others, out of Shannon's reach. Chance gingerly picked it up with a handkerchief Marco offered from his breast pocket. Shannon lost all control and began to wail and blubber incoherently.

Amelia finally got hold of whatever she had been searching for and jumped up, slowly stalking toward Shannon with pure hatred in her eyes. "You killed Bo, you bitch!"

I realized Amelia was holding an old-fashioned meat thermometer. It was pointy and looked lethal. I stepped between Amelia and Shannon. "Amelia, put down the thermometer. It's over." I looked back at Shannon. "She's over."

Amelia stared at me, her lip trembling and tears spilled down her cheeks. "I can't let Bo go unavenged, Kat. He was everything to me." She looked down at Shannon with disgust. "Prison is too good for her."

I took another step closer to Amelia and put my hand on her arm. I looked at her sincerely. "You're right, Amelia. Prison is too good for her. She deserves so much worse." I took a deep breath. "But *you* don't deserve to go to prison, Amelia. You have too much to live for, too much that you still need to do in life. Your kids need you." Amelia's hand started to waiver and I continued. "I remember back in high school, you always talked about running for office and changing the world." I gently took the

161

thermometer out of Amelia's hand and passed it back to my friends. "It's not too late. And Harmony is about to have a special election for mayor." Amelia collapsed against me as the swinging doors crashed open again and Ty charged through, followed by three of his officers.

Ty looked at each of us, clearly confused. Shannon was crying on the floor. Amelia was bleeding and hysterical. Chance was holding a bloody knife with a handkerchief and apparently Ricky was the lucky recipient of the scary-looking thermometer that I had handed to him. I was, once again, covered in blood and tears. Nothing new there. Syd caught her breath and pulled Ty over to the side to quickly explain the events of the last fifteen minutes. He listened quietly and nodded occasionally. Finally, he motioned the officers toward Shannon. They put her in handcuffs and Mirandized her as they escorted her out of the kitchen.

Chapter Thirty-Five

Once again, the ambulance came racing up to the resort, sirens wailing. First, the paramedics attended to Amelia's arm. They determined that the gash would need stitches and loaded her onto a stretcher. They looked surprised and concerned when they saw me and the copious amounts of blood covering my clothes —again—but I assured them that I was uninjured this time.

Ty sent each of us away with a different officer to collect our statements. By the time I finished with Officer Freely, I felt like I had been beaten up, physically and mentally. The final luncheon had been canceled under the circumstances, and the rest of the reunion guests had been allowed to check out and leave, so it was just Syd, Ricky, Marco, Chance, and me sitting on the patio. We were voraciously eating pizza that had been delivered shortly after Shannon was arrested. It turned out that right after breakfast, Shannon had told the head chef that Mayor Brad wanted to cater the last lunch and give the kitchen staff the rest of the day off with pay after all the chaos of the weekend, which was why the kitchen had been empty. She knew Amanda would show up to oversee this last event and this way she could be sure to catch her alone. I couldn't figure out why Shannon had actually ordered the salad and pizzas from Tuscan Pizzeria, but we were all grateful for the food. Maybe Shannon thought it would bolster her alibi or earn Mayor Brad a few more votes when he ran for state legislator.

Ty stopped by and told Syd he would be home late. He pulled a face and made a comment about bureaucracy and paperwork. He kissed Syd on the head and asked if she could pick up the kids at his parents on her way home.

She smiled up at him and said she couldn't wait to see them after this past weekend. Housekeeping had generously packed up all our belongings and brought them down to the lobby. Ricky had said they probably didn't want to risk us getting any more blood in the room.

Syd stretched. "I'm going to go right now and leave a *very generous* tip for housekeeping after the messes we made and with them being so nice to us."

I reached in my pocket as we all headed into the lobby, but Syd waved me away. "We'll work it out later. We'll figure it out." Syd looked at Ricky and joked, "He's not getting away without putting in his share. I'm tired of supporting his lazy butt, with all his money."

Ricky smiled disarmingly. "What? I never carry cash." He spied one of his Robotics Club friends out in the parking lot, packing up his car. "Hey, there's Santos. I want to offer him a job." Ricky knew that Santos was brilliant and had been working at gig jobs way under his skill level. Ricky also liked to help people out and Santos could use the help. He had two kids at home and a third on the way. He ran off to the parking lot with a wave and a hurried, "See you later!"

Syd waggled her fingers at me and went rushing over to Ty, standing by a bunch of luggage and starting to pick up a couple of suitcases. "That's Kat's, not mine," she called. Ty shook his head in exasperation and pointed toward another suitcase with a raised eyebrow. Syd nodded.

I continued walking with Chance and Marco up to the lobby to retrieve my belongings. I stopped and asked hesitantly, "Will I see you both soon?"

Chance and Marco looked at each other and back at me. I blushed three shades of red and both men chuckled.

164

Marco grinned. "Well, I'm sure I'll see you and Ricky at The Mercury." He snorted as he laughed at the look on my face and then looked a little nervous. "Oh, well, uhm, I guess now is as good a time as any."

Chance elbowed him. "Spit it out!"

Marco took a breath. "Okay. You know how I said I could tell when people know their wine and have a good palate? Well, I know you really like wine, Kat," I gave him an affronted look and he laughed nervously. "You know what I mean—you're knowledgeable and you enjoy it. Well, I'm starting a new division of Milano Fine Wines that will focus on wine tasting events to expand our customer base and help us sell more wines to distributors and independent liquor stores." He looked at me apprehensively. "I was hoping you would come to work for me. Head up the new division."

I stared, dumbfounded and speechless. "Uh, that's something I never thought about before, Marco." I looked around for Syd or Ricky, but neither was in sight. "Can I have a few days to think about it? And I think I'd like to know a bit more about the job before I decide."

Marco jumped up. "Of course. Let's meet for lunch on Tuesday and I can give you more details and we can flesh out my vision."

"That sounds great! Okay, lunch on Tuesday." Marco gave me a quick hug then started to walk away with a swagger. I still looked stunned and called out, "Marco?"

He turned around.

"Thank you for thinking of me and for the offer!" I smiled at him.

He grinned back at me. "No problem. I only want the best in my business." He then blushed a little and he turned to walk toward the hotel lobby.

Chance stretched his arms over his head and I found my eyes traveling up his body with impure thoughts running through my mind.

165

Chance caught me watching him and chuckled. I blushed once again and Chance ruffled my hair.

"I should get a move on, too," he said. "My sister has been dealing with the renovations of the bar on her own all weekend. Who knows what design decisions she made while I was away?" He smiled at me. "Did I tell you she likes mermaids? The whole place will probably have an underwater theme with life-sized mermaids if I don't rein her in." He turned to walk away.

I cleared my throat nervously. "Chance?" He turned around with a half-expectant smile.

"Yes?"

"You never answered my question."

"What was that?"

"Are we…" I paused. Stop being such a chicken. "Am I going to see you again soon?"

Chance slipped his arm around me in a half-hug. "Well, I'll be easy enough to find. I will be spending most of my waking hours at Two Cups." He then nervously cleared his throat. "In fact, I was hoping you could come to Two Cups and help me work out the wine list for the opening. Is Thursday good for you? Around 5? We could try out the kitchen at the restaurant too, make sure everything is working properly."

I looked at him silently for a moment and he rushed to cover the silence. "I hope it won't be too awkward for you to come to your mother's old bar. I hope to see you there a lot." He looked a little embarrassed. "Syd and Ricky, too, of course."

Had he just asked me on a date? I smiled up at him and grinned back at me. "I'd love to come on Thursday and help you with the wine list as well as test the kitchen."

Chance visibly relaxed. It was kind of funny, seeing him so nervous about asking me out, kind of. Chance cleared his throat. "I'm glad you've decided to stay in Harmony, Kat. Until a few minutes ago, I thought you were planning to leave."

I looped my arm through his and started walking toward the exit. "Before this weekend, I was still thinking about getting out of here." I looked down the hill and out over the town. "I never realized how much I really had worth staying for." Was that a tear in my eye? Geez! "I never realized how genuine and nice the people still here in Harmony are." I smiled. "If I lived here, I think I could get used to that."

About the Author:

Thank you for reading *Reunions Can Be Murder*. Please join Kat and all her friends in the next installment of *The Wine Tasting Mystery Series,* due in later this year.

Tammy Wunsch currently resides in the Quiet Corner of Connecticut though she has also called both New York City and Los Angeles home. Formally educated in business, she has worked in a variety of industries and is both entrepreneurial and adventurous by nature. She is passionate about animals and loves to travel, cook, kayak, and read.

Where can you see everything that Tammy writes and in which she is involved?

1. Look for more books and her blog at TammyWunsch.com

2. She publishes The Copywriter Agency – a learning portal and online job board exclusively for Content and Copywriters.

3. Stay in touch. I love to read comments, suggestions, and reviews.

Bonus #1:

I would like to formally invite you to participate in a *Wine Tasting Mystery Series* Community Wine Tasting Project. This project is to develop a wine tasting database by everyday wine drinkers. While some of you may be experts, most don't know a whole lot about wine but still enjoy the delicious taste. Let's see how our ratings compare to the experts!

Use the link below to complete tasting and rating information that will be shared with other readers. I will provide a monthly update on my Tammy Wunsch, Author Facebook page. I look forward to seeing the types of wines and ratings. This form may someday turn into an app, but I'll let you know when that happens. https://forms.gle/pAmkVRahVa6z68P69

Like and follow my page to stay updated on what I write and on our Community Wine Tasting Project.

Bonus #2:

I have attached Wine Tasting Notes following this page. Feel free to copy or print these pages for your own personal wine tasting notes. You can file them by location, type of wine, or…?

Plan your own wine tasting with friends and distribute the notes so you can compare at the end.

Happy reading and *Á votre santé*!

Wine Tasting Notes

Vineyard Name/Wine Producer:

_____

Name of Wine and Variety:

_____

Vintage Year: (Circle)

2020	2019	2018	2017	2016	2015	2014	2013
2011	2010	2009	2008	2007	2006	2005	2004
2002	2001	2000	1999	1998	1997	1996	1995
1993	1992	1991	1990	1989	1988	1987	1986
1984	1983	1982	1981	1980	1979	1978	1977
1975	1974	1973	1972	1971	1970	1969	1968
1966	1965	1964	1963	1962	1961	1960	1959

Do you like this wine?   Yes. No. Unsure   Would you buy this wine again?   Yes No Unsure

Personal Wine Rating (0-100): _____   Wine Glass Rating Scale: (Circle) 🍷 🍷 🍷 🍷 🍷

Wine Growing Region:

	Country	Region/State/Area		Country	Region/State/Area
◯	Argentina		◯	Moldova	
◯	Australia		◯	New Zealand	
◯	Austria		◯	Portugal	
◯	Brazil		◯	Romania	
◯	Canada		◯	Russia	
◯	Chile		◯	South Africa	
◯	China		◯	Spain	
◯	France		◯	Ukraine	
◯	Germany		◯	United Kingdom	
◯	Greece		◯	United States of America	
◯	Hungary		◯	Other	
◯	Italy				

General Wine Type:

◯	Red	◯	Sparkling
◯	White	◯	Port
◯	Rosé	◯	Dessert Wine

Personal Wine Tasting Notes:

Reunions Can Be Murder – The Wine Tasting Mystery Series (Book 1): Wine Tasting Notes

Wine Color: (Choose One)

	Pale	Medium	Deep
Amber			
Brown			
Copper			
Garnet			
Gold			
Pink			
Purple			
Ruby			
Salmon			
Tawny			
Yellow			

Wine Bouquet or Aroma: (Circle up to 5)

Apricot	Caramel	Honey	Nutty	Raspberry
Asparagus	Chocolate	Leather	Oak	Smoky
Bacon	Coconut	Lemon	Orange	Straw
Banana	Coffee	Lime	Peach	Strawberry
Black cherry	Eucalyptus	Licorice	Pear	Sulphur
Black pepper	Fig	Lychee	Pine	Tea
Blackberry	Grape	Melon	Pineapple	Toasted bread
Blackcurrant	Grapefruit	Mint	Plum	Tobacco
Burnt toast	Grassy	Molasses	Prune	Vanilla
Buttery	Green pepper	Mold	Raisin	Yeast

Wine Flavor: (Choose up to 5)

Apple	Chocolaty	Leafy	Oaky	Raspberry
Apricot	Cinnamon	Lemon	Oily	Smokey
Asparagus	Cloves	Lime	Oranges	Spicy
Banana	Cranberry	Lychee	Papaya	Strawberry
Blackberry	Currant	Mango	Passionfruit	Sweet
Blueberry	Earthy	Melon	Pear	Tart
Burnt	Fig	Mint	Peppery	Toasty
Buttery	Flowery	Musty	Pineapple	Vegetal
Cedary	Grapefruit	Nectarine	Pruny	Watermelon
Cherry	Grassy	Nutty	Raisiny	Yeasty

Reunions Can Be Murder – The Wine Tasting Mystery Series (Book 1): Wine Tasting Notes

Made in United States
North Haven, CT
11 November 2021

11045993R10102